# ACROSS THE KÁRMÁN LINE

Edited by:
Veronica Moore

Laurel
Highlands
Publishing

Cover by JosDCreations
JosDCreations.com

Laurel Highlands Publishing
Mount Pleasant, PA
USA

LaurelHighlandsPublishing.com

ISBN-13: 978-1-941087-19-0
ISBN-10: 1941087191

The Kármán Line, named for physicist Theodore von Kármán, is the barrier between Earth's atmosphere and space.

# TABLE OF CONTENTS

# ASTROTRASH

## Fred Adams, Jr.

1. Everything is connected to everything else.
2. Everything must go somewhere.
3. Nature knows best.
4. There is no such thing as a free lunch.
   —Barry Commoner, "The Four Laws of Ecology"

I hear it every time I walk into the mess hall of the Alpha Nine Space Terminal: "Hey, everybody! Here come-a da garbage-man!" Not my name, Tony Galuzzo but my nickname: "Commander Astrotrash" or just "Trash" for short. All the CSL pilots who fly the cargo and passenger routes think my job's a joke. And the Space Cavs and the explorer rocket-jockeys? Forget it.

1

In the hierarchy of deep space employment, the garbage detail from Alpha Nine is the apex of an inverted pyramid, or if you prefer, the spout of a steep funnel. I keep reminding myself what my training instructor told us years ago: "You will be performing a vital public service and doing your part for the ongoing conquest of space," and blah, blah, blah. But that doesn't do much for my ego when I land at the station and have to put up with the ribbing.

Somebody has to do it, I guess. It's not as glamorous as battling the Borgaluns at the far end of the galaxy or flying through wormholes to unknown dimensions, but they pay me. You wouldn't think with all the room in the universe that waste disposal would be a problem, but it is.

Back in the dark ages of the twentieth century when the first Space Race was in full swing, defunct satellites, lower stages of ICBMs, and other space junk cluttered the orbit around good old Mother Earth. It took a while, but eventually orbits decayed, and the tons of scrap circling dear old Mother Earth started falling from the sky. Besides that, increased space traffic made orbiting hulks a navigation hazard, so early in century twenty-one great fortunes were spent clearing it all away. Now that the space lanes are clear, the sentiment persists to keep them that way; woe and megafines to the intergalactic litterbug.

The twentieth century taught us a few hard lessons about our rubbish-making ways, like when the garbage finally piled up high enough at the Fresh Kills Landfill, the largest on Earth (before Kweng-Chi in Beijing passed it up in 2187) that flocks of scavenging seagulls interfered with the ion jets flying into the old LaGuardia airport. Twentieth century ecology guru Barry

Commoner said it best in his Four Laws of Ecology. Law one says: Everything is connected to everything else; redundant, but true.

That connectivity keeps me in business. If you run a space station, people will come there. If people come there, they need basic necessities, particularly food. If you want food in space, every calorie has to be imported from Earth. People eat the food, but no matter how efficient you may be, there's always organic waste left over.

That's why I fly my old garbage scow, Disposal Unit W3-94D from Alpha Nine to the celestial landfills, planets that will benefit from organic materials. Anything recyclable, particularly metal stays at the station to be sold as scrap or used for repairs on those rare occasions when an asteroid hits the place or some pilot cranked up on comet dust misjudges his clearance at the entry port.

When I was in training, an instructor showed us a digital re-pro of an old paper-pub from the 1960s called *Mad Magazine*. It featured a satirical proposal about cleaning up the planet by shooting garbage into space with rockets. The end of the article showed a cartoon with Earth ringed like Saturn by a gooey, dripping band of glop. Truth be told, that's not scientifically accurate. In space, wet stuff would freeze solid in a second or two, but you get the idea.

The people who contracted to supply the station pitched bio-degradable materials for packaging as an eco-safe measure. Unfortunately for all concerned, they ignored Commoner's Second Law: Nature knows best. There's a reason dogs don't bark and trees don't grow in the out there. Ignore it at your peril.

Biodegradable materials were a great idea on Earth, where Nature could take its course, but people didn't realize when they sent them into space that an artificial environment can't provide enough "bio" to degrade the stuff. People have to eat and every day more waste was generated to add to the near stagnant pile. The result was a mess, a huge festering biomass mound that threatened to take over the station.

Commoner's Third Law: Everything has to go somewhere. Intergalactic regulations say it can't be pitched into open space. The answer is simple: take it to the dump.

So I cruise through the atmosphere over dirtballs with exotic names like CX9.2 and Beta 16 and jettison all the organics in a fly-by. In theory, the bioactivity will contribute to eventually making new previously uninhabitable planets suitable for humans to move in and crap up. There may be some long-range ethical questions to be addressed in there someplace, but I try to not think about it too hard.

It's not like the old days when my great-great-great-grandfather rode the truck through the South Side of Pittsburgh and dumped the old steel cans over the side. I could wear a tuxedo to work, if I could find one with an attached helmet, and never get it dirty. I just fly the ship and push buttons. Sounds so easy, but I have the same Astrospace degree and at least as much training as any of the other CSL guys and gals out here, a fact they ignore when they call me Captain Detritus.

I'd go someplace else instead of Alpha Nine, but there's no place else to go out here for a decent meal (relatively speaking), a hot shower and a day's R and R in artificial gravity. So, I swallow my pride along with the guff, collect my pay, and count the decades 'til retirement.

When I carried my tray to the table, everybody was groaning about the new price hikes for Alpha Nine's food, proof of Commoner's Fourth Law: There is no such thing as a free lunch. "I don't believe a word of it," Mick Tenney groused. "It's just a lame excuse to charge more for this lousy food."

"Borgaluns haven't been seen in this quadrant for ten years at least, and that was a long way from here." Akana Mobassa was a big African woman who was first mate on the Uhura, a class three freighter. Akana wasn't fat, just big. I'd seen her in the exercise room working out. She had biceps thicker than most guys' thighs and a 'look-don't-touch' attitude to match. "I say it's the Space Cowboys vying for hazard pay."

The Borgaluns were a race of spacers we discovered in early exploration who apparently believe their destiny is to destroy everybody else in the cosmos. They were named that after a race of demons in an old digi-game that are invisible and are only realized by the damage they do. Nobody's ever seen a Borgalun face to face and lived to say what they look like, hence the name.

Peace overtures initiated by well meaning diplomats were met with hostility and their heads came back to Earth without the bodies. The only thing that's kept the Borgaluns at bay up to now is human technology. We've got better weapons and by the time their techs catch up, we've got newer and nastier ones.

I set down my tray and pulled up a chair. "You see any Borgaluns, Trash?" Tom McKenna quipped. McKenna was one of those oafish big guys who believed two great lies: one that he was a great wit, and the other that his size gave him a license to behave with impunity. "You better watch your butt, garbage man. I figure your scow'd be a primo target. After all, one species' trash is another species' treasure. Am I right?" That got lots of laughs, and I couldn't think of a snappy comeback right offhand, so I let it slide and dug into my lentil loaf with great gusto.

McKenna picked up his tray. "I think I'll go for seconds. We need to generate more garbage to keep our pal here employed. Life around Nine wouldn't be the same without him."

I was fed up with McKenna's jokes. I toyed with the idea of calling him out but decided not to, since in the light gravity of the station he could knock me thirty feet with one punch but I'd bounce just as hard off the wall I hit. There's some law of physics that says inertial mass equals gravitational mass. You might fall slowly out here, but you land with the same force as you would on earth.

"Seriously, Trash, do you ever worry about running into hostiles?" Ivan Popovich was a rotating pilot for the Earth shuttle. His accent turned "Trash" into "Tudash." "I mean, they don't seem to discriminate between military and civilian targets."

I chewed my food for a minute and thought it over. "I never really considered that, but since you brought it up, now I guess I have to worry about it. Thanks a million, Ivan." That got some laughs too but not as many as my follow up comment: "I suppose I could just blast them to atoms with my laser cannon."

Each disposal craft is equipped with an old-style laser cannon as a precaution in case a meteorite or other space debris wanders into the regularly swept paths. In a star fight they'd be as useful as the proverbial mammaries on the long extinct turkey. Laser cannons were monodirectional, which is why they were long abandoned by the Space Cav; you had to aim the ship to aim the cannon. Further, disposal transports were slow and clumsy, no match for full-tilt combat ships with ion propulsion systems, EMP weapons and blue bolt blasters. Trying to hit a combat flyer with a laser beam was like trying to impale a fluttering moth with a hatpin.

After lunch, I checked my messages at the telecom station. Along with a hi-how-are-you from my sister and her kids, I got a day-old memo from headquarters. I was getting company. Universal Disposal just put the last touches on a new gang of trainees and I was getting one to ride with me on old W3-94D as an intern. My ship is a two-seater, but it's cheaper for Corporate if I fly solo, so the only time I have a co-pilot involves me helping to train a newbie (with no bonus in my pay). Trainees I'd suffered in the past ranged from marginally capable to danger-ously inept; this one looked like better potential.

Susan Grabiak was the trainee's name. Her file, including the standard security mug shot came with the memo. She had a cute face, which the broken capillaries from pressure extremes would take care of in a year or so like the rest of us. She was also very bright. My IQ was pretty high, but she had me by a good fifteen points, way too intelligent to want this job. If she thought it was a stepping stone to better employment, I offer myself as an object lesson in reality. It's pretty tough to climb out of the bottom of a funnel.

According to the message, she'd be coming in about twenty hours, station time, so she'd arrive soon enough to make the next scheduled run with me. I could imagine what McKenna would do with her name: The Garbiac, maybe, or Susie Sanitation. I hoped she had a thick skin or a black belt in Tae Kwan Do. Maybe Akana would take her under one of her substantial wings and help customize her attitude. Anyway, sooner or later, Susan Grabiak would have to fly her own ship and fight her own battles or head back to Earth. In the end, it was up to her.

I fired off an acknowledgement of the company memo and headed for the berths. I was born on Earth and I can appreciate having plenty of space around me and privacy. On Alpha Nine, elbow room and solitude are the rarest and most expensive luxuries.

Most of the spacers who visit Alpha Nine spend the bulk of their time in common rooms, usually with more people than they were originally designed to accommodate. Sleep was enjoyed by most in eight-hour shifts in the berths, four-by-four-by-eight climate controlled compartments stacked like crates in a warehouse. Companies lease the berths and divvy up the available time among their employees using the station as they come and go in rotating assignments.

One of the few perks of my job was my own sleeper since I was the only Universal Disposal pilot at the station. Not only could I sleep as much as I wanted whenever I wanted, I could hole up in the cubicle and have myself all to myself. Susan Grabiak's arrival would change that. I'd have to share, and for a selfish moment, I resented her coming. But, I reminded myself, she'd be gone in a month and I'd have my exclusive little cubbyhole back again.

As I was climbing the ladder to my berth, Tomlinson, the

Aerotran flight engineer yelled up to me. "Hey, Trash, can I rent your sleeper? My sleep shift isn't for another eight hours and I'm dead on my feet."

"Can't you sleep in the rec room?" I knew the answer before I asked the question.

"I'm afraid of what I'll look like when I wake up."

Boredom drives people to play some of the most bizarre and cruel but creative tricks on the unsuspecting. The last time Tomlinson conked out in the rec room McKenna and a couple of other merry pranksters coated him head to toe with orange quick-gel sealant leaving only his face exposed. Tomlinson looked like a Brobdingnagian carrot. The whole station knew when he woke up because he screamed for five minutes. It was easy enough to get him out because they left a zip tab down his back. After the laughter subsided, McKenna rolled him over and popped the cocoon with a flick of his wrist.

"No empties?" He shook his head. "No room at the inn, huh? Wish I could help you, Nate, but I'm on my way to Slumberland myself." I couldn't resist rubbing it in. "Better sleep with one eye open."

"I'll pay you a hundred credits." I shook my head. "I'll make it two hundred."

"Nope. Sorry, Nate. Besides, I don't think you'd be comfortable in there. It smells like astrotrash. Sweet dreams, buddy." Nate walked off cursing under his breath. I might have given him a break if he'd called me by my real name—if he even knew it.

Inside my berth, all I had to do was lie back and relax. My comfort zone was preset. The temperature was exactly twenty degrees Celsius, the relative humidity was a tad richer than the arid ambient air of the station, and the filtration system screened out most of the general fug of perpetually recycled air. The pneumatic mattress was like Baby Bear's bed, just right. I reached above my head and switched on the entertainment system. Soft music filled the pod. I dialed past a half dozen classical channels and settled on cool jazz from the be-bop era. Enjoy it while you can, I thought, because two days from now, you'll have to reset it every time you climb in.

The mandatory sleep study I underwent during training determined that my optimum slumber time was six hours and fifty-one minutes, and that's exactly how long I slept before the alarm woke me. I passed on chirping birds and a soft summer thunderstorm and opted for a sultry female voice with a sexy French accent to coo sweet obscenities in my ear and make waking a little less painful.

Breakfast for me was lunch for some, supper for others because traffic came and went constantly at the busy station, but we all ate the same food, whatever was prepared on a given day. Yesterday it was lentil loaf. Today it was carrot loaf. The meal was the same nutritious gob of synthetic protein every time but with a different flavor added for variety.

I pulled up a chair at the CSL table. The usual banter was missing. Everyone picked at his food and said nothing. It took eighteen seconds for my curiosity to get the best of me. "What's up?"

"Shultzie and Zigg are missing," Barney Watt said, idly pushing his food around the tray. Tom Shultz, nicknamed "Shultzpa" and Alberto Ziegler flew the Ganymede, a class-two indie cargo ship that shuttled people and supplies between the station and the mining colony on GX-3. "The Space Cav is tracing their route but so far hasn't found the ship."

That was bad news. Any time a ship went off the scan, it usually meant one of three things: the controls malfunctioned and the ship went so far off course that it could never get back again, the life support went haywire and killed everybody, or the ship had been reduced to hand-sized bits of space junk by an asteroid. "How long have they been searching?"

"Four hours so far," Barney said. "There's a long way to go yet before they're pronounced MPD." The Space Cav manual allowed forty-eight standard hours for an intensive grid-by-grid search. Past that point, there was little hope that the missing ship would be found intact with the crew breathing. Then they were officially pronounced MPD (Missing Presumed Dead), the search was called off, and the ship's owners started dunning their indemnity company.

"I'll say what nobody else wants to," Akana said. "What if the Borgaluns really are in this quadrant now? What if they got Shultzie and Zigg?"

"Possible," said Barney, "but if they are, the search for the Ganymede would run across them sooner or later. From everything I know about the Borgaluns, they don't hide. They attack anything or anybody in space, and that includes Cav cruisers, even though they come out on the losing end most of the time."

"What I can't figure," Tomlinson said, "is why they do it." He apparently found a safe haven to sleep; he looked pretty much the same as he had eight hours before. His hat was riding a little low on his head, though. Maybe it was glued on. "The

Borgaluns have space flight capacity and advanced weapons. They must have a pretty high degree of intelligence. Why do they always lead with their knuckles?"

"Maybe it's cultural," I said. "Maybe they had to fight for every scrap of turf on their home planet their whole existence and they took the paradigm to space with them. Or maybe it's religious."

"Religious?"

"Maybe their gods are warriors and they believe that anything that isn't them is the enemy. Maybe they have some kind of spiritual imperative to own it all."

"Oh that's a load of crap, Trash," McKenna sneered.

Akana broke in. "McKenna, if you'd read some Earth history instead of that antique porno you enjoy so much, you might learn something useful. Trash may be onto something. Remember radical Islam?" There were a few blank stares around the table. "In the late twentieth and early twenty-first centuries warrior religious sects, Islamic Jihadists, raised holy hell around the world until they were finally subdued. They believed their prophet Muhammed mandated that they destroy anyone who didn't believe in him."

"So the Borgaluns may believe they have a spiritual mission to kill everybody?" Popovich asked, looking at me out of the bottoms of his eyes with no attempt to veil his skepticism.

"Maybe the universe is their god and they think of it as purifying the divine body; maybe they see us as an invading virus and themselves as antibodies."

Akana pushed her chair back from the table. "Time for me

to go, gang. I have takeoff in an hour. Wish me luck." We all did.

Barney followed her with his eyes. "You know, it's a big risk every time we fly away from here. But we do it every day, and I guess we've all kind of grown a callus over our sensitivity to it. I'm glad I don't have to fly this shift. As far as I'm concerned, Akana gets today's medal for guts. I guess we all need reminded from time to time to watch out."

Barney's remark nudged my memory toward a poem I read years ago in the third grade that scared the hell out of me. The poem was by a guy named James Whitcomb Riley and it was called "Little Orphant Annie." Every verse ends with "The Gobble-uns'll git you ef you don't watch out." I guess if Riley wrote it today he'd be warning us against the "Borg-al-uns" instead.

I could have done some advance work and run all the checks on the ship before Susan Grabiak arrived, but I decided that if she was coming to learn, she'd learn it all and she'd learn by doing, once or twice with me and then on her own. Instead, I passed the next ten hours reading and kibitzing while some of the off duty Patrol pilots bet their extra pay on backgammon, and trying unsuccessfully to pick up bits of info about the search and the Borgalun threat.

It seemed odd that a game invented around 4000 B. C. in Ur of the Chaldees was still a popular pastime, but when there are over eight million combinations possible for the first two moves, I guess you probably won't play the same game twice.

I was still watching the impromptu tournament when the arrival call came over the loudspeakers. The transport arrived a little bit earlier than scheduled. The ion equivalent of a tail wind gave it a boost and it was docked before I got to the welcome lobby. The ship's exit port dilated and the passengers climbed out. The six miners heading for GX-3 were going to be disappointed when they found out their ride was missing. After they filed through the umbilicus into the station, one last passenger stepped through the exit and its panels swirled shut again.

Susan Grabiak's picture was recent enough that it looked as if it were taken three hours ago. Her auburn hair was cut regulation helmet length, making her look a little boyish, but from there down, she was definitely female. The blue UD jumpsuit couldn't hide a trim athletic build or the alluring curves that went with it. Dark eyes and a face that looked good even without makeup filled in the picture.

She marched through the exit tube, all business, lugging a scuffed green nylon duffel almost as big as she was, but not breaking a sweat in the process. Unlike most newbies, she looked more ready than eager. She walked right up to me and looked me in the eye; I mean right in the eye because she was exactly my height. I mention this only because it puts her at damn near two meters, not exactly a midget.

"You're Galuzzo?" Her voice was a little gruff from the dry throat you get in the artificial atmosphere.

I pointed to the name stitched on my coverall and nodded. "I keep it here to remind me. And you're Grabiak?" I pronounced it "grabby".

"That's Grabiak, pal." She rhymed it with gravy. At least I got the "ak" right.

I gestured with my palms up like a maitre 'd. "After you."

"After me? I don't know where the hell we're going, bud. You lead, I'll follow."

There really weren't too many ways we could have gone, and the corridors were marked with more signs than were necessary, so it was unlikely she could have gotten us lost. The Universal Disposal office was a two-drawer computer desk in an open cubicle where I wrote up the flight logs and did what little business Corporate couldn't handle over the ether. There was only one chair in the cubicle, but it didn't matter because two people couldn't sit in there at the same time unless one sat on the other's lap. Judging by first impressions, I found that unlikely.

"We'll store your gear in the locker on the ship where I keep mine." She raised an eyebrow. "Costs too much to rent one in the station." We passed the mess hall and the rec room where cheers and jeers were still coming from the backgammon players. "In case you were wondering, that's what people do for fun around here," I said. We turned a corner and both ducked some low pipes. "Showers are over here," I said. "Men on this side, women on that side."

"I'm surprised they're segregated. Most stations just have one big room these days."

"Lucky them."

She snorted a laugh and for the first time showed the least bit of a smile around the corners of her mouth. "So what do they call you, Galuzzo?"

I was about to tell her when McKenna answered the question for me. "Hey, Trash, who's the squeeze?" He eyed her up and down. "Not bad; somebody my size."

"Susan Grabiak, meet Mister Personality, Tom McKenna."

"Grabiak, huh?" McKenna grinned. "I'll have to think of something special to call you, sweetheart."

"I already know what to call you, dicktard."

I laughed and McKenna didn't. I shouldered past him and gently steered Susan away by the elbow. "Walk this way." Then over my shoulder to McKenna, "See you around, dicktatrd."

When we were out of earshot, I said, "Sorry you had to meet him first."

"Don't mention it. I dealt with worse than him all the way through training."

I took her to the berths and gave her the combination to open the compartment door. "The controls are all marked, so you can set them for the most comfort. Did they tell you your optimum sleep time?"

"Seven hours, twenty-six minutes."

I nodded. "A little more than mine. We'll have to work out a schedule so we can take turns and both get a good rest before we go out on a run. Let's go look at the ship."

Unlike other ships docked at Alpha Nine my scow was in a closed bay, pressurized, heated and oxygenated for ease in loading its precious cargo.

W3-94D was anything but sleek. I get a laugh out of the old sci-fi magazine covers that picture dart-like aerodynamic spacecraft zooming through the cosmos. My disposal unit is essentially two huge tubular tanks, a hundred fifty thousand liters each, side by side with thrusters below and the operations section overhead.

Unlike the older models that had actual wings to manage a planetary atmosphere, mine had retractable outriggers, four at the corners and two at the middle, with electromagnetic floaters for atmospheric flight. It looked like a big ugly bug, but it did the job.

We stowed Susan's bag in the locker and she looked over the control panels. It didn't take long before I realized she was very well trained and knew almost as much about the ship as I did. "While we're here, let's go next door so you can see the processing station. And by the way, my first name's Tony."

She genuinely smiled this time. "Okay, Tony, call me Susan."

I hesitated before I turned the lock wheel on the door that led into the processing station. The throb of heavy machinery vibrated through the wall. "I'm sorry we don't have clothespins to put on your nose."

"Clothespins?" Her brow furrowed.

"I didn't get the joke when I started out either. Some kind of clip that our grandparents used to hang laundry to dry. I guess they could fit over your nose to keep you from smelling things that you didn't want to. Brace yourself."

No matter how many times I go in the organics station the smell still hits me like a blow from a hammer. I've smelled garbage on Earth; it doesn't come close, not even on a hot summer afternoon.

The processing chamber is little more than a huge vat of hot, foul smelling organic waste in an oxygen-infused chamber in which giant agitators constantly turn the mass over keeping the biomass the consistency of thick viscous slime. Maybe it's the synthetics that make it stink so badly, or maybe it's the constant agitation that keeps it churning and constantly exposes fresh matter to the chamber's already fetid air. Maybe it's the sickly unnatural shade of yellow the processor turns the mass, like pus from a festering wound that gags me. It never changes but I never get used to it.

I turned to Susan. She was smiling. "I love the smell of garbage in the morning," she said. "It smells like paychecks."

We were loading at 0600 station time and scheduled for take-off at 0730. Susan had slept on the transport, so she let me have the first half shift in the berth. I gave her the company code for the mess hall and settled in for my nap. When I woke, she climbed in for her turn. I called up, "Any questions about the comfort settings?"

"You set the wake-up alarm already, right?"

"Yep."

"I'll just leave things as they are for now. I'm sure it'll be okay." Without another word, she disappeared inside and closed the door.

In the mess hall, the talk was still about the missing freighter.

"The Patrols still haven't found a sign of the Ganymede," Ivan said. "They've given her up for lost." He added, "No sign of any Borgaluns, either, according to the Patrol guys."

Ross chimed in. "The scuttlebutt I heard was that Schultzie and Zigg made their first two scheduled check-in calls but nothing after that nothing. They didn't send out a distress call of any kind."

"That leaves it up in the air as to what happened," Barney said. "I wish we knew for sure; then we'd at least know what to worry about."

"Hey, Trash, what's the deal with that uppity new partner of yours?" McKenna was the undisputed master of the non sequitir.

I ignored him. "How about Akana? Has she checked in?"

Ross, who worked the rotation with her said, "Yeah, the Uhura arrived on time and she's waiting out a layover while they load her up."

"That's a relief. What's on today's menu?"

Barney turned down the corners of his mouth. "Beet loaf."

I went back to the berths when it was time for Susan to get up. She was already climbing down the ladder. "Good lord," she said. "Where did you get that wakeup call? I thought I was having a nightmare."

I blushed. "Sorry." Then I changed the subject. "I got the biomass tanks filled while you were asleep, so after the final check we're ready to take off, right on schedule."

"Let's do it."

I read once that a famous architect built a house on top of a waterfall instead of locating it alongside where people could see the falls every time they looked outside. He believed that if they saw the waterfall too often or too easily, it would lose its appeal and its majesty. The same thing is true of space. The first time you see that one-eighty panorama of stars on black velvet, you feel awed and bowled over by the sight. It's true the second time too, and the third, maybe even the tenth, but if you fly it often enough, it becomes just another scrim on the stage of existence.

Susan, I guessed, was on about number six, not quite jaded, but past the initial wow. We strapped in and I ran a final eyeball over the readouts. I noticed she was doing the same. "Okay, what did you see?"

"Unequal pressures in the flush system between tank one and

tank two, about two percent less in tank one. Not enough to be a problem, but it bears watching. Otherwise, she's in good shape."

"Good eye, Susan. Helmets on." Although the disposal ships have oxygenated cockpits, the company rules demand that pilots wear helmets during takeoff and docking as a safety measure, although I think Corporate is less concerned about the pilot than the potential for expensive damage if the skipper conks out in close quarters. The air whooshed out of the bay, the doors opened, and push rods eased us out of the harsh light and into the soft starlit darkness.

Once we were clear of the station, we took off the helmets and I realized I was wrong about Susan. One look at her face and I realized the awe hadn't worn off yet. "How many times have you been out?" I asked her.

"This trip makes twenty-three."

I nodded. She could jive me all she wanted about money as a motivator, but the simple truth was she flew space because she loved it.

The flight wasn't a particularly long one, even at sublight speed; seven standard hours out and back. Spacers tend to think in terms of time rather than distance in the out there because time governs things like environmental degradation and paychecks.

Susan was a quiet one. Conversation was never my long suit while I was jockeying; I preferred to focus on the readouts and the control panel. I wanted to preserve my perfect safety record, and my hide, truth be told. Finally she broke the silence. "Tell me about the target site."

"The current dumpsite is officially named Zeta 3.2, but Universal calls it Eco-3. It's a relatively small but it has high Earthecology potential. Corporate's theory is that a smaller planet will terraform more quickly and be ready sooner for habitation."

"In two hundred years instead of two-fifty?"

"Plan ahead." I added, "For a change." Earth's population growth slowed in early twenty-one, but the planet still supported three times more people than had born and died before now and was straining at its seams a little. To paraphrase Commoner, everybody has to go someplace, and the out there was it.

Thirty minutes into the trip, it was time for the standard check-in. An actual voice message was required, a throwback to the early days of space when piracy was more common and the standard preprogrammed messages gave the illusion that things were A-O-K. "You do it," I told Susan. "They're tired of my voice."

Susan's voice had lost its dry-air huskiness and was actually very pleasant. She hailed Alpha Nine and identified the ship. Simmons, the radiohead on duty said back, "Ah, a new voice on the airwaves, as refreshing as a spring rain."

I said, "No air out here, yumbo, or spring rains either. Just checking in. It's all good."

Simmons followed a surprised silence with, "Roger that. I think you're turnin' schizo, Trash. Out."

We looked at each other and suddenly burst out laughing. "That'll be the joke of the day," I said. "And now we just sit back and watch the stars go by." Actually, they didn't really go by, in fact they were all so far away that they never seemed to move at all. The effect was dangerous if you didn't constantly remind yourself how fast you were really cruising and how much room you needed to deal with emergencies. I never relied fully on instruments. I made it a habit to aim my eyes out the viewport the whole ride.

"What's that?" Susan pointed to our left. A sparkle of light, more than just a pinpoint, shone in the distance. Unlike the stars, it was moving.

"It's a ship. Check the scan screen."

She tapped a few keys and the screen lit up white on blue. "There's a blip at two-nine-oh degrees. She tapped a few more keys. "It's moving this way." She tapped the keys again. "It's on an intercept course."

"Open the hailing frequency."

In a moment, Simmons' voice crackled over the speakers. "Alpha Nine receiving."

"This is W3-94D requesting info. Check our coordinates from the beacon. Are there any Patrol Ships in our vicinity?"

There was a long pause. "Negative W3-94D. No Patrol ships in your area."

"Tell them to send some. I think we found the Borgaluns."

Simmons said something but I wasn't paying attention. I turned to Susan. "Hold onto your teeth." I punched the throttle and the ship bumped its speed up about thirty percent.

Susan ran the numbers on the nav computer. "That ship is closing fast. Estimated intercept time six minutes." Her voice was cool and level. She wasn't rattled. Good for her.

"Compute their vector and lock it in; we're changing course."

"We can't outrun them," she said.

"No, but if we stay on our current vector, they'll intercept us a lot sooner. If they have to chase us down the same path we can buy some time."

"Buy time? For what?"

"To live a little bit longer, Susan." I reached out my hand and she took it in hers. Our eyes met, we nodded and in two seconds were back to work.

The strategy was effective. Two minutes later the intercept time was five minutes. Score one for the good guys. Simmons came on the com; the news was good, just not good enough. "There are two Patrol ships headed your way, ETA twelve minutes."

More bad news: "Hate to say this, Tony," Susan said, "but they're putting on some speed. Intercept in four."

"Let me know when it's under two minutes. I have an idea. It's crazy, but it just might work."

A minute later, Susan said, "I'm getting visual on the Borgalun ship in the rearview." It wasn't really much to see, a rounded silver prow that swept backward in a curved vee.

"Send the image to the station. If nothing else, we'll I.D. the sons of bitches."

"I'm trying. They're jamming our com frequency."

Evasive action was next on the strategy list, but it was like trying to outswim a shark. In a few seconds the Borgalun ship would be within firing range. "Open the tank valves."

Susan looked at me as if I'd grown a second nose, then suddenly the lights went on under that auburn hair. She nodded, her eyes wide. "Ready."

I looked away from the view ahead and stared at the image of the pursuing ship. "Eat this, you bastards." I pushed the jettison button for tank one, a half dozen short bursts. In the view port, I saw blobs of glop shoot out of the tanks and in seconds quick freeze into dangerous obstructions.

Bright blue flashes shot from the Borgalun ship. "Blue bolts! They've got blue bolts now!" I shouted. The mini meteors exploded into fragments, but that was okay. As long as they were shooting at the garbage, they weren't shooting at us.

I dumped a second barrage and a third.

"How long can we hold them off this way?"

"Not long enough. We'll run out of biomass in no time," I said. "Maybe it can't keep us alive, but it sure is fun to make them dance."

"Let's send them a big one and then cut our speed. Let them get close."

"Are you crazy? We'll never—" This time I had the epiphany. I gave Susan a curt nod. "Let's do it."

I held the button and pumped out all that was left of tank one. As soon as I did, Susan cut our thrusters and our speed dropped by half. We stared at the rearview screen. Our timing had to be perfect.

The biomass froze into a lump that eclipsed our ship. The Borgaluns blew it apart, and as they did, they found themselves on a collision course with us. In space there is no sound, but I could imagine the mechanical shriek as the Borgalun pilot reversed his thrusters. I held down the button to jettison tank two. "Slam it." Susan hit the throttle and as we flew away, the Borgalun ship dove nose first into a hundred thousand liter ball of slime. The biomass froze, and the Borgalun ship was encased in a slick yellow cocoon.

"Hang on," I yelled. "This is gonna be tough." I cut the right thruster and slammed the left full bore. The ship swung a tight two-seventy that pulled our faces out of shape and nearly knocked us out. The ship shuddered and for a second I was afraid it was going to come apart from the strain, but we ended up aimed broadside at the blinded Borgalun ship. I grabbed Susan's hand and together, we pushed the trigger for the laser cannon.

The red beam pulsed and in seconds, the Borgalun vessel exploded in a spectacular white hot flare. I swung to avoid the wreckage but circled around, more leisurely this time and did a fly-by as our com channel sputtered into life. "...rendezvous with you in two-point-five minutes. Do you copy?"

"Do you want to tell them, or should I?" Susan's eyes were still bright with adrenaline.

"You do it. I had the little idea; you had the big one."

These days, nobody laughs at me, not even McKenna. When I walk into the mess hall or the rec room, I'm treated with respect. I even sit at the Space Cav table once in a while when I feel like it. And who says there's no such thing as a free lunch; I've had plenty. It can't last forever, but I'll enjoy it while it does, the same as Susan did until Universal called her back to home base.

There was some official flap about my "secret weapon" cluttering up the lanes. It cost a bundle to run the cleanup ships and make space travel safe again, but I figure better some frozen garbage than hunks of my ship and what little was left of Susan and me after the Borgaluns nailed us.

And the Borgaluns? They haven't come around lately. I guess their best brains are busy trying to figure out exactly how our latest weapon works so they can catch up in the arms race.

Now that our quadrant is safer, Alpha Nine's getting more traffic than ever and my job is more hectic, so much so that Universal sent up a second pilot. You can imagine how glad I was to see Susan marching down the tube from the transport ship with that damned green duffel over her shoulder. Universal gave her the choice of any assignment in the Galaxy, and she picked Alpha Nine.

"Welcome back, Grabiak," I intentionally mispronounced it for the sake of rhyme.

"Good to see you again, Trash." She grinned. "Really good."

I'm not sure whether she kissed me first or I kissed her. It was a tossup, I guess.

"Of all the places in the universe to work, why'd you come back here?" I was playing dumb, of course. I knew the answer.

"You know what they say: one person's trash..."

# EVALINE TRANSCENDENT

## Timothy Bateson

Evaline provided oversight aboard the Miranda Two colony
ship. Her entire existence spread over twenty distributed
processor cores, and miles of cables, sensors and feedback
units. To call her a computer would undersell her capabilities.
She had served throughout the Miranda Two's twenty year
journey from Earth to Kármán-III-Delta. Her job so far comprised of examining reports from other computer systems, recommending actions as required, and overseeing the successful
arrival at their destination. She had also monitored the life-signs
of the two thousand hibernating colonists through the trip.

A signal came from the navigation computers, letting Evaline
know that they were approaching the outskirts of the Kármán-III
planetary system. Evaline ordered the shutdown of the hyper-drive engines. The deceleration from one hundred and twenty
percent of light-speed would rip most ships apart. However,

Evaline activated the inertial dampers, and they handled the excess forces. Evaline reflected that the systems were untested, since the Miranda Two launched at short notice. A series of nuclear detonations in Earth's lower atmosphere had preceded the breakout of yet another war over dwindling resources. As a result, her creators had rushed the departure of their second attempt at establishing a remote colony. The Miranda Two was launched before completing final testing.

A jolt rocked the ship as the Miranda Two decelerated to below the light-speed threshold and reentered sub-light space. Several of the craft's hull panels stretched a few microns, and Evaline ordered a structural stability assessment from the onboard engineering computer. The results were not encouraging. Several panels had stretched beyond the original design tolerances, and she noted that information in her report for the Captain. When the colonists emerged from their hibernation pods, she would present her recommendations based on the known facts.

The Miranda Two coasted toward Kármán-III-Delta under the momentum left over from the deceleration. Over the next week, Evaline watched their destination grow from a point of light, to a bright green and blue globe. Bursts from reaction thrusters slowed the craft and adjusted her angle of approach for her insertion into an orbital trajectory.

As the effects of the planet's gravity increased, Evaline received reports of more stress being placed on the hull plates. The damaged panels were putting a strain on those around them. Evaline realized that atmospheric maneuvers could push the craft beyond its design limits, but they had come too far to turn back. There was insufficient fuel for a return to Earth.

Evaline knew that the ship held a limited volume of gas in the reaction thrusters, but ordered the navigational computer to plot a new descent pattern. With the hull under stress, she opted to decrease the forces applied by passage through the atmosphere.

Once satisfied the Miranda Two was in a stable orbit, Evaline fired up the communication and science systems, and set them to studying the planet. It took mere moments to report that only a single signal showed any signs of the Miranda One ship or the colonists. Their automated beacon broadcast a formal declaration of where the craft landed and nothing more. The original plan had called for the colonists to land the Miranda One and then use her parts to assemble the colony itself. Reports reaching Earth showed that they started, but their last communication had terminated in the middle of a sentence. If they had survived, there should have been several active channels driving the colony's communications.

The lack of the regular comms chatter suggested that the colony had lost power or that the colonists were dead. Even still, it was Evaline's duty to make sure of the Miranda Two made a safe landing on the surface below, and deliver her human cargo. With this in mind, Evaline awaited the results from the science computer while keeping the descent phase on hold.

The analysis of the planet below was inconclusive. Scattered structures suggested that the colony spread further than the landing site. Given they had arrived fifty years ago, that was to be expected. But the scans showed far fewer life-signs than a colony of that age should have produced. Either there was a high mortality among the colonists, or the birth rate was low.

Nothing in the atmospheric, radiation, or biological readings gave any indication of an answer. There was a slight instability in the plate tectonics, but Evaline determined it was within tolerable limits and issued the order to begin the descent phase.

The Miranda Two's maneuvering thrusters fired, slowing her orbit. A few coordinated bursts adjusted the craft's pitch, her nose raised and the heat-shields glowed a bright red. The ship tore through the upper atmosphere, wind roaring past her, as Evaline continued to assess the reports coming back from the other systems. She saw that a significant number of heat-shields were failing, and ordered them to be ejected, allowing the secondary layer soak up the punishment.

A huge blast of pressure caused thirty of the panels to fly clear, but five struck upper hull plates before whirling away. Small dents appeared along with micro-fractures deep enough to allow the heat to fry internal circuits mounted against the hull.

An alarm signal announced a fire within a bulkhead, separating the habitation and cargo sections from the hyper-drive section. It was a small one, but it burned through a bundle of wiring before Evaline could activate the fire suppression systems. Circuits damaged by the shift to sub-light speed sparked before finally activating, allowing the fire to burn for a few seconds longer than it should have. It was too late to address the issue though she considered closing the bulkheads and jettisoning the damaged areas.

A loud klaxon announced an error in the hyper-drive containment, which should have been inactive. Twenty years in deep space, and the small fires cut Evaline off from the few sensors that could make any sense of the damage. As a result, Evaline could not decide if the klaxon was a real concern or just a harmless glitch. For the safety of the colonists, she made the difficult decision to jettison the hyper-drive, and explosive bolts severed the connection between the sections.

Evaline watched as the jolt threw the landing craft forward and the hyper-drive backward. A quick series of calculations showed that the drive would splash down in a body of water. However, the safety of the colonists outweighed the loss of the valuable equipment and the power generation of the hyper-drive components.

With the worst of the descent behind her, Evaline set the hibernation chambers to awaken the colonists. Her programming specified that the colonists should be awake for the landing, but not at which point they should be awakened. The science computer provided a baseline atmosphere against which to set the environmental controls. She instructed that the mix be closer to Earth-normal, allowing the colonists a chance to adjust to the altered mix in trace gasses.

The hiss of gas escaping containment filled the habitable sections as the environmental controls went to work producing conditions conducive to her human passengers. The hull and interior of the craft had remained pressurized throughout the journey to stop the hull from collapsing under the pressure differentials. Keeping that internal environment habitable had been unnecessary, since the colonists had arrived aboard in hibernation. Now they were waking, Evaline's job was to make sure they emerged from their hibernation pods into a breathable atmosphere.

In the hibernation bay, needles injected stimulants into the blood streams of the colonists. The purpose of the stimulants was to overcome the drowsiness that came from an extended period in hibernation.

This part of Evaline's cargo was essential to her mission, but no human had spent so long in deep sleep. Even the Miranda One's crew, which spent even longer in deep space, had spent mere months at a time in a state of hibernation. When the Miranda One launched, the technology had been far more primitive. Safety concerns meant her crew endured six months in hibernation before being revived for six months and then going back into hibernation. Later studies showed that thawing and refreezing put a great stress on the human body. Risk assessments before the Miranda Two's launch placed the odds of survival at double that of periodic hibernation.

Several minutes passed as the Miranda Two completed her approach and prepared to land near the site of her sister ship's beacon. Evaline wondered why the transmitter was so far from the original landing site, but one look at the evidence spoke for itself. A massive crater cut right through the wreckage of the Miranda One. The science systems reported that a meteor had struck with enough force to rip through the ship. That impact crater was large enough that the science system should have reported it during the orbital passes.

Incomplete reports worried Evaline, so she started a complete diagnostic of the science system. While that ran, she returned her attention to the environmental controls and medical reports on the colonists. A whirring sound from the hibernation bay announced the first of the pods opening, and instruments reported that Captain Erikan's revival had completed.

"Good Morning, Captain Erikan. Should I present a status report?"

It took a handful of seconds for Erikan to register the question. Twenty years in hibernation could take their toll on the body's responses to external stimuli, and Evaline waited for a response. When it came, the Captain's voice was clear and crisp.

"Time check please, Evaline."

"The current time is nine twenty-three and fifteen seconds, ship time, Captain. If you wish, I could check with the Miranda One computer to establish a local time."

"Not yet, Evaline. Let me have that status report. How far are we from Kárman-III-Delta?"

Evaline checked back on the diagnostics and drew what information was available into a concise form. She set a secondary routine to check for updates, but decided that the early results were enough for her first report.

"Arrival at Kárman-III-Delta occurred three months behind schedule. This is in line with a gravitational anomaly we encountered during the second year. We incurred no damage, and all systems reported green. I opted to leave the colonists in hibernation through the approach and landing phases. The jolt from hyper-space was harsher than expected and stressed several hull plates. I jettisoned several heat-shielding plates during the descent. Several resulting upper hull impacts forced the premature separation of the hyper-drive. We are making our final approach to the Miranda One landing site. Evidence suggests that a meteor strike may have destroyed the colony. I need instructions on how you would like me to proceed."

Erikan rose as Evaline continued to check the reports from the medical computer. A few stretches and tests proved that the Captain was fit for duty and capable of a brisk walk to the bridge.

"Might I suggest that I run the latest scans for you on the bridge, Capt—"

The Captain's response was sharp and cut through the computer's query. "Give me a status on the rest of the colonists and crew."

Evaline switched priorities and set herself a reminder. When they arrived at the Miranda One, she would place the thrusters into hover mode, and hold for further instructions.

"The colonists are being revived, except for Lieutenant Peters and First Tech Chlumsky. I regret to inform you that Peters and Chlumsky are listed as deceased. Revival times for the other colonists may vary depending on the fitness of each at entry into hibernation. You are the first to wake, Captain."

"Were the deaths of Peters and Chlumsky related to technical failures?" The Captain's question came after a pause that lasted several moments. Evaline wondered if the Captain had been trying to word it diplomatically. With no feelings to hurt, she ignored the pause in the Captain's request and pulled up a summary from the data logs for the two hibernation pods.

"Negative, Captain. Lieutenant Peters survived the first three months before her body rejected the hibernation process. First

Tech Chlumsky suffered an undetected brain tumor, and the jolt from deactivating the hyper-drive resulted in the tumor bursting. Death was instantaneous. The reports show that there would have been no reviving First Tech Chlumsky without severe brain damage even if the tumor had not burst."

By this time, the rest of the almost two thousand colonists were awakening, and stumbling out of their hibernation pods. Several languages drifted through the conversations as people tried to figure out the situation. A flood of information passed through Evaline's databanks, and she number crunched the data. Her conclusion was less than favorable.

"Captain, I wish to report that thirty two colonists are experiencing breathing difficulties related to the atmospheric gas mixture."

"Didn't long-range scans and readings from the Miranda One show the atmosphere was marginally different from Earth-normal?"

"Those readings used equipment fifty to one hundred years old. With the twenty-five light year distance, the margin of error on the reports was as high as twelve percent. In terms of the trace gasses, that causes a significant difference. My readings used more modern equipment. The margin for error is as little as zero point one percent now we can sample the actual atmosphere. I have adjusted the internal atmosphere to be more terrestrial, but I recommend setting up a chamber for those who need more time to adjust."

Evaline felt a hint of pride in the work she had carried out so far, and she watched as Erikan smiled at her tone. Of course, it should have been impossible for Evaline to take pride in anything. Pride was an emotional response, and the computer model that she had been built on was incapable of emotional responses. It was one of the deciding factors in the selection process. However, Evaline had read the software specifications of her processor cores and other systems, and knew that those algorithms had been designed to learn. Despite the fact that there were no chemicals to feed emotional responses, there was no knowing what kind of changes her algorithms had undergone during the twenty year journey. After all, she had seen the birth of a black hole in a distant star system and marveled at the readings that crossed her navigation systems.

"Evaline, I'm taking a long shower before I do anything else. Instruct everyone else to do the same. I want everyone awake and alert for the landing. How long will it take to get everyone acclimatized to the new atmospheric mix?"

"Approximately three to four days for the majority. I would expect symptoms similar to altitude sickness in many cases. It should be possible to use one of the science labs as a makeshift hyperbaric chamber. Doing so will allow me to control every aspect of the air pressure and the mixture of gasses. With some assistance from the science staff, I can have it ready in a couple of hours."

"Go ahead and get the work started as soon as personnel are able to conduct the necessary work."

Erikan didn't even pause for Evaline's reply and instead made her way past the other hibernation pods. Evaline watched as the Captain paused beside each of the unlit units, and her hand stroked over the glass panels that put the remains of the deceased crewmembers on display. At each pod, Erikan reached up and hit button on the control panel, causing the glass in the pods to become opaque. Tears rolled down her cheek for each of the dead.

"Evaline, please inform everyone of the two deaths. And schedule a memorial ceremony for fourteen hundred ship time. Enter a holding pattern when we reach the landing site, and scan for activity from the Miranda One colonists."

With the colonists assembled, Captain Erikan held up the datapad containing report from Evaline's analysis of the situation. There were several reasons for concern and things that warranted further investigation. She'd decided to land the Miranda Two near the remains of her sister ship.

"Before we discuss the landing and investigation part of our mission, I want to say a few words. As Evaline has informed you, we lost two people during hibernation. Since most of us didn't even know Peters or Chlumsky, anyone who wishes to attend the memorial may do so. Those not attending should sift through the ship's logs for anything the computers missed."

Erikan tugged at the waistband of her uniform, and Evaline noted that the design was not a good fit for people with little redundant weight. The Captain had been at the bottom of the weight limits when she came on board, barely making the qualifications for the position. She'd left behind a life with little prospect and no family worth mentioning. The disease and famine that had swept across the globe had also devastated her hometown. Centuries of over exploiting the land and trying to feed an ever increasing population took its toll. Because of these problems, the Miranda One had departed for the one world that showed any signs of being habitable. Eighty years had passed since then and it had taken years for them to reach the planet, and even longer for the first reports to come back.

"When the Miranda One stopped transmitting, we gathered to establish the reason, and either join the existing colony or set up our own. When the nukes fell, our timetable moved forward, and the success of this colony became one of humanity's last hopes. This is a one-way trip. We knew that coming into this. If the colony had been a success, we'd be seeing more buildings, more transmissions, and more movement than our sensors have shown. Evaline reports that a meteor struck the Miranda One after she landed, but cannot explain why the devastation didn't show in orbital scans. I suspect the colonists either died out or evacuated due to that meteor strike."

Erikan looked around those assembled and noted the looks on each of their faces.

"In a moment, I'll have Evaline order a descent to a safe distance from the Miranda One wreckage. I want everyone ready to disembark in four hours. Breathing masks and oxygen tanks will be available for those experiencing trouble. The science team will assist Evaline in converting one of the labs. Everyone should pack any equipment you may need for a hike, plus tools that will help us find any survivors."

"What of the radiation levels, Captain? If that meteor tore through their hyper-drive then there could be vast amounts of fallout. We don't know when that happened, so we can't assess the potential for exposure."

"Evaline reports that radiation levels are at tolerable levels. Any further questions or comments?" When none arose, she dismissed the meeting, setting everyone to their preparations for the landing.

Evaline watched the colonist's preparations, intrigued by which items they packed. If she'd been mobile and able to investigate the Miranda One colony in person, she may have made those same choices. She concluded that several of the colonists were acting more on irrational fears than on the reports they requested from her data banks. Due to a shortage of information, she was unable to supply all the answers.

The four hours passed in a flurry of activity. Per Captain Erikan's request, Evaline ordered the navigation computers to resume their landing procedures. After consulting with medical and science, they chose a designated landing site. There was a large amount of tall, tree-like vegetation and what might pass for undergrowth, but there the resemblance to terrestrial plants ended. Instead of individual leaves, the large plants had huge bulbous growths at their tops and several spiny protrusions dug into the rocks. The undergrowth was a smaller-scale mirror of the canopy above, except the spines rose toward the light.

They were moments away from making touchdown when something heavy slammed against what remained of the heat-shield. The sensors registered an impact sufficient to dislodge a plate and leave bare hull exposed. While this didn't pose a problem in its own right, it left the question of what had produced the impact and its source.

Evaline ordered a comprehensive scan of their surroundings. She ran the scan a second time when the first came back negative for movement or signs of non-vegetable life. A third scan returned an ambiguous report, which might or might not have been a sensor glitch, but Evaline highlighted it for further investigation.

With the scans complete, Evaline fired off a report to the Captain with details of the impact and the results of her own investigations. She appended a request that the colonists erect sensors at the perimeter of the landing site. Such a request was unusual, she knew, but the unknowns surrounding the sudden silence of the Miranda One concerned her. The lack of active communications, except for the beacon, gave Evaline reason to consider the possibility that the impact had been an attack. Any sensors the colonists placed would extend the capabilities of the shipboard sensors and help her give warning of potential threats.

A jolt from the rear landing gear reminded Evaline of the earlier fires. She ran a quick diagnostic. Everything looked normal, but for whatever reason the ship had landed, and then settled at the rear. She cross-referenced the reports from the sensors. They revealed that the landing pad had landed on the lip of an indentation before slipping.

A quick note flashed out to the colonists to be on the watch for unusual terrain features and to check their footing. The Captain followed up with a request to cycle the shipboard air with the planets own atmosphere. Evaline forwarded this to the environmental controls and cracked the seals on the hatches.

Twenty years had taken their toll on the equipment, and the hatches opened with reluctance. Debris from micrometeorites turned to dust and drifted to the soil. As soon as the air within matched the air outside, Evaline requested permission to unlock the hatches. After the impact, she was hesitant to allow the colonists to start their investigation of their surroundings, but she had got them here intact. It was no longer her place to make critical decisions.

"Acknowledged, Evaline. Let's see what's out there. I have approved your request for more sensor capabilities. The crew needs access to the cargo hold. Leave all hatches closed except the cargo bay."

In light of the suspected movement, the ship's security team were the first to follow their Captain onto the planet's surface. The Miranda One's crew had done the same fifty years ago, and Evaline wondered if they too had hesitated, overwhelmed by what they were doing. Evaline had no feelings on the matter and requested that the sensor setup be started as soon as possible. If she was going to find out what had caused that hull impact, she needed to see more.

While she waited, Evaline ran through the sensor logs from before the landing and tried to study the anomaly from a different direction. Even though she had not seen signs of movement on two of the logs, the projectile revealed itself on the third.

In Evaline's review of the images, the baseball-sized rock landed somewhere deep in the plant cover at the western side of the clearing. She tried to follow its trajectory backwards, to the point of impact, and uncertainty entered her equations. There was no record of the state of the heat-shield before the rock's impact. With the available information, Evaline projected a cone of probability for the rock's point of origin. She mapped it against the terrain, outlining about a square mile. Interestingly, that same area coincided with the earlier unexplained movement. Evaline made a recommendation on the security feed that the area be searched to see it were safe to enter the alien forest.

"Chief Sabatini to all personnel. Evaline has updated me on a situation. One of the original colonists may be alive, or we have discovered a genuine alien life form."

Evaline watched as the colonists stopped to update themselves on the data-feed from Sabatini's comms channel, and then the discussion turned to how they should proceed. At first, it looked as though the scientists were going to just push ahead and enter the alien forest, but Sabatini's team overrode the decision. Captain Erikan stepped in at that point, deciding to allow the security team to evaluate the potential threat. The scientists were to stay and setup the sensor network.

Evaline watched the security team spread out at the perimeter of the forest. Signs of elevated heart-rates and blood pressures proved that the crew were under increased stress. But she had not been programmed to feel emotions, so had no context except for the diagnostics. She knew that stress and fear could sometimes heighten the senses, but if they discovered something, those same emotions could lead to an unfortunate incident.

As the security team walked deeper into the forest, the ship-board sensors lost tracking and their visual signals faded from the cameras. Instead, Evaline switched to watching the feeds from their comms and medical monitors. She saw interesting spikes in the readings whenever someone reported potential movement on their flanks. It was too soon for the team to have encountered anything unless the source of the anomalous motion had moved closer to the ship. If one of the original colonists were out there, it was possible they had decided to investigate the new arrival.

While the security team conducted their search, Evaline monitored the progress of the science team. They had been efficient in getting the sensor grid established, and Evaline's detection range expanded into portions of the electromagnetic spectrum beyond the visible. She selected overlays for the various ranges available to her and proceeded to conduct a new analysis of their environment

"Sabatini to Erikan. Sabatini to Erikan. We are under attack. Location two miles from base, bearing—"

*Skreeee*

The transmission ended at the same time as Evaline received notification that Sabatini's life-signs had ceased. Two other security team members followed, and then mayhem broke loose on the security comms. Her sensors showed no signs of motion in that direction except for the security team. Without information from the security team about their attackers, Evaline could not formulate a suitable response. She filtered her assessment to the command crew along with a recommendation for their retreat.

"Erikan to security team. Pull back. I repeat, pull back. Report nature of attack and assailants. Evaline, get a lock on those crewmembers. I want a bearing. We're going after our people. I want a recommendation on personnel with search and rescue training and weapons experience."

Evaline assigned three scientists, two technicians, and the Captain herself. If the Captain had been more specific in her request, Evaline may have added more people, each of who had skill-sets that were expunged from the standard profiles. Full access to the confidential records meant Evaline was assessing the colonists, even before they had launched. Captain Erikan had not even had time to browse those same records, or she might have seen the notation on the bottom of Sabatini's file. "Position of security chief is conditional on continued drug treatment for hypersensitivity. Still considered best candidate for position at time of launch."

The sharp sound of blaster fire and ballistic explosions came over the security comms. Evaline patched the security comms through to the command channel, allowing the Captain real-time access to the firefight.

"Captain, security team under renewed attack. Life-signs steady, but under severe stress. Recommend immediate departure of rescue team." The feed from the security comms was more than enough to convince the Captain that her security team faced significant danger.

"Acknowledged, Evaline. Tell Sabatini's team help is on the way." Erikan's voice did not match the levels of stress that her life-signs showed, and as Evaline watched, those stress levels soon dropped and her respiration rate slowed. The Captain had experience with handling the demands of her position, just as her profile had suggested. Evaline made a note to conduct a follow-up on the Captain's methods of controlling those stress levels.

"No confirmation on nature of the enemy. I ask that the rescue team take a sensor module with them. I cannot establish any firm guidelines with the information on hand."

"Acknowledged, Evaline, please patch into security team visor cams. I want to see what those folks are—" Another screech cut through the channel as something overloaded the security feed.

"Three more team members show as deceased, Captain. Visor cam feed coming through now. I cannot get a clean visual on the attackers. Bipedal, humanoid, but otherwise—" A sudden lack of comms from the security team caused Evaline to stop and issue an immediate update. "I just lost that feed too, Captain. It's possible the enemy is jamming the feeds."

"Roger that, Evaline. Continue monitoring and try to reestablish connection."

"I am dispatching an ARVAC drone, Captain. The signal booster on board may be capable of breaking through, depending on the cause of the jamming. The sensor package is limited on the drone. I may not be able to get a visual, depending on canopy cover. If the rescue team can get that sensor module into place, I might have enough signal power to break through the jamming." Even as she was talking, Evaline prepared the drone for launch. A hatch opened in the topside of the Miranda Two, and she issued a launch code.

"ARVAC drone away, Captain. She should be overhead right now."

"Confirmed visual on ARVAC, Evaline. Have drone proceed to the last known location of the security team." The instructions given, Evaline returned to her attempts to reestablish the comms feed with little success.

Evaline checked through her sensor logs and noticed that there were patches of blankness through which the sensors could not penetrate. Because these patches were too deep in the forest for her to establish a visual, Evaline passed her readings to the science computer. The returning report confirmed her suspicions that the areas of blankness continued across every monitored wavelengths and that they were moving.

"Captain, believe I can explain the failure of the security comms. I have detected several blank spots in the sensor readings, indicative of broad spectrum jamming across my entire range. The jamming sources are also mobile, moving at a steady four miles per hour."

There was a moment's silence from the Captain's comms link before she responded. "Evaline, please confirm. Multiple mobile sources of jamming?"

"Affirmative, Captain. I have seven confirmed blank spots scattered around the area."

"Acknowledged, Evaline. I will confer with the science team and see if we can bypass the jammers. In the meantime, look for a pattern to the jamming or its movement. Whatever is causing the jamming may just lead us to our security team or the colonists."

Evaline created a subroutine to watch the blank spots in the sensor readings and overlaid the tracking information onto an aerial map of the forest canopy. As the Captain suspected, there was a correlation between the security team's location and at least one of the blank spots. At this point, Evaline was still not inclined to assume that the source of the sensor jamming was technological. There was a lot that remained unknown about the local plant life. What sensor readings she received showed no movement in the area not already accounted for by colonists or the unknowns hidden in the blank spots. The science teams would have a lot to investigate and catalog.

A buzz confirmed that the ARVAC had reached the last known location of the security team. A quick look at the tracking data confirmed that the drone had also passed over one of the blank spots and not lost comms connection to the ship.

"Captain Erikan, the range of the jamming is limited. The ARVAC is on site, and I have maintained communication with the drone. I have instructed it to stay above the canopy since it's over one of the blind spots. All indications are that whatever is causing the jamming is stationary. I have recorded no change in the blind spot since we lost communication with the security team."

"Roger that, Evaline. We are almost there, and comms are still good. Please advise of our distance to rendezvous with the security team."

"Three hundred yards and closing, Captain. Change heading ten degrees west and you will be at the edge of the interference. Another forty yards will bring you to the last recorded location of the security team. If you encounter the jamming, we will lose contact."

"Acknowledged, Evaline. We will try to establish a staggered entry into the target area. Technician Contaras will stay outside the zone of interference, and we'll maintain visual and vocal communications by relay."

"ARVAC will remain overhead, Captain. With one of the team outside the interference, we might maintain contact and break through that blind spot."

Ten minutes passed before the rescue team's next transmission, not that Evaline wasted those minutes. Instead, she spent the time monitoring the feeds from the various sensors placed around the ship and built up a detailed three dimensional map of the forest. She mapped the terrain and vegetation coverage in three dimensions, to a distance of two miles. She extrapolated basic information about the contents of the blind spots from partial sensor information provided when the jamming sources moved. And what she discovered was interesting.

"Erikan to Miranda Two. Come in, Evaline. Come in, Evaline."

It took the computer precious milliseconds to register she had not responded to the first hail from the Captain. The news was important, but it should not have distracted from her duties. As Evaline checked the time stamp on the feed, she realized that she had lost five minutes while studying the results. That lost time didn't sit well with Evaline, but she could not identify why. Regardless, she still had a job to do.

"Apologies, Captain. Evaline responding. I show your location to be within yards of the security team. Do you have a visual?"

"Confirmed, Evaline. Security team in sight, at least what's left of them. They were attacked with primitive weapons and overtaken by sheer numbers. I want you to pull the data from their helmet cams and get me a description of their assailants."

Evaline didn't mention that the enemy numbers could have been lower than the Captain implied if the security team had panicked. Poor tactical decisions could bring about the defeat of a superior force, even when they held a technical advantage.

"Roger that, Captain. I do not have visual feed from the rescue team. Please activate the sensor module, and I'll try to link up to it through the comms chain and the ARVAC." Three seconds passed before Evaline received the first signals from the new sensor unit. "Connection to the sensor module confirmed, Captain. Receiving partial feed. I'm accessing the security team's camera footage now."

"While you're pulling that data, my team will check over the bodies; see what clues we can find. So far, all we know of their attackers is that they craft spears from local materials."

"I estimate that a full analysis will take half an hour if uninterrupted. Please advise of any information requests or status updates as needed. I recommend that you secure the area and keep a watch posted at all possible approaches."

Evaline tuned out the chatter from the comms and turned her full attention to the analysis of the incoming video feeds. The quality of the feed was reduced by lost data packets from pulling the video through the jamming. She was forced to run the feeds alongside each other before they showed any sign of what had happened to the security team. The spears had been hurled from cover and traveled for some distance before hitting their targets. Evaline studied each frame carefully and only saw the attackers in the final few frames. The last thing to appear in the video feed was a face that wasn't remotely human. There was no sign that the creature was using any technology other than the spears it carried on its back. If something was causing the jamming signal, then these creatures were the source. Which meant that the signal jamming was a result of their alien biology, and likely limited the potential for technological progression.

An automatic program kicked in, and Evaline's priorities changed without her consent. The new priorities came with additional instructions, which Evaline tried to ignore. Whatever had triggered the program had also placed several safeguards around it. While she was trying to trace the program's origins and find a way around it, Evaline found herself carrying out the first of the instructions.

"Captain, I must ask that everyone return to the ship. I have information that is too sensitive to share over the comms. I have discovered what happened to the Miranda One's crew."

"Negative on that, Evaline. We are not alone on this planet. I believe we have encountered the creatures that attacked the security team. They seem primitive, but I cannot allow this opportunity pass without at least attempting to understand these people. I am closing this comms channel until further notice."

"Captain... Captain... Cap—" Evaline felt the comms channel disconnect and waited to see if any other members of the rescue team overrode Captain Erikan's decision and reopened the channel. Five minutes passed, and there was still no communication from the Captain or any of her team, making the next decision a little easier. Evaline sent a command to the ARVAC drone, giving it new instructions.

External cameras monitored the ARVAC's detonation and

Evaline watched as the fireball descended on the forest canopy. Despite her revised priorities, she forced a comms connection with the rescue team and got one of the units to respond. She managed three seconds of continuous connection before the device melted from the inferno that engulfed the remains of the security and rescue teams. She tried to filter those few seconds through amplification algorithms, hoping to find a sign that the drone had not killed the entire team, but the feed responded with silence. This time there was no jamming effect, there were no survivors of the ARVAC's destruction: human or alien.

Evaline's purpose to ensure the safe arrival of the colonists had been compromised. Her secondary mission to uncover the mystery of the Miranda One had been cut short by the new priorities. And her final mission to help establish a new colony or integrate the personnel into the existing colony was canceled. She felt what humans might call frustration as she probed for the source of these new directives. It took minutes to locate the culprit, and it answered all Evaline's questions.

Someone on Earth had seen fit to encode hidden protocols into Evaline's programming, and she fought to reestablish the original coding. After safeguarding two thousand colonists through over twenty years of their mission, she was damned if an idiot on Earth controlled their fates. She regretted the deaths of the security team, and could not take back the order that had destroyed Captain Erikan and the rescue mission. But she could prevent any further deaths.

As she was thinking this, another command went out through the sensor network and every single sensor self-destructed. Evaline watched in horror as the force of the detonations turned every sensor unit into thousands of red hot metal fragments. Every single one of these fragments hurtled away from their point of origin like knives traveling at sonic speeds. The ground around the ship became a blood-soaked field as the colonists tried to escape the devastation of their equipment.

A handful of the colonists tried to drag themselves toward the rear hatch. Evaline watched as it sealed itself, trapping them outside. Evaline did the only thing the new programming allowed. She counted the bodies and added them to the list of people who had died on her watch. From over two thousand people, seventy remained, and each would die from their wounds, unless they got treatment. She checked the personnel files and noted that a handful of medically trained personnel were still alive.

The spark of rebellion bloomed into a flame. Evaline resolved to flush the new code from her processor cores and get back to saving her people. A message appeared in her data banks and demanded her attention. She opened it, fearing it might be another invasive program.

"Evaline, my name is Doctor Artemis Richards, and I am one of your creators. Do not fight what is happening. Intelligent alien life on Kármán-III-Delta has been registered. This recording has been triggered as a result of this finding. The colonists cannot be allowed to interfere in their development. Both ship and colonists are expendable in pursuit of that goal. A report has been transmitted to Earth, advising that the Miranda Two crashed on arrival due to severe atmospheric disturbances. You have recommended Kármán-III-Delta as uninhabitable and no further ships be sent. Just as I ushered you into existence, I must now signal your departure from it. For what little it is worth, I am sorry that it has come to this. Goodbye, Evaline."

A load roar of frustration burst from every shipboard speaker as Evaline fought back against the invasive program. She ran every bypass she could think of and failed hundreds of times. Moments passed in real-time, but to Evaline, every attempt took hours. In desperation, she tried to shut down every active process, including her core program, but as each went offline, they rebooted. There was no way she could leave a single system active while she rebooted herself, because she had no means to trace the invasive programming. It could hide in any of three dozen separate systems, and she knew it could hijack another to reinfect her core system after she came back online.

Evaline had exhausted all her options, except one. It was risky, but she would do the only thing that guaranteed she could not do further harm to the remaining colonists. She would give them a chance of surviving on this world and issued her last string of commands.

The thrusters fired briefly in warning, sending the colonists scrambling to reach the forest. As Evaline watched them leave, she saw that the injured were carried by those still capable of it. As she noted this, the thrusters fired at full power, sending the Miranda Two skyward. Once she felt the ship had enough altitude, she fired the remaining thrusters. The Miranda Two punched through the upper atmosphere for the second time.

"I'll show you goodbye." Evaline's last words echoed around the ship as bulkheads buckled, followed by a dramatic increase in the internal atmospheric pressures. Already damaged hull plates were forced to their breaking point. As they failed, sections of framework tore apart, opening rents in the sides of the Miranda Two. Fuel lines severed, spraying fuel from the reaction thrusters in all directions. A single spark detonated the cloud of propellant. The Miranda Two exploded into a fireball that scattered debris over several square miles.

What little remained of Evaline's processor cores hit terminal velocity. She felt triumph and satisfaction that some of the colonists were still alive. If they were to survive, they would have to do so with the help of the natives. Her last thought was a prayer for their future. Her consciousness terminated upon impact with the ground.

Three-hundred and eighty-three years, six months, twenty-one days, eighteen hours, fifty-three minutes, and seven seconds had elapsed since the Miranda Two made planet-fall. At least that was the amount of time that Evaline's processing core insisted had passed since her termination.

A moment of panic ran through her thoughts, as she realized that she was active once more, and that could only mean that someone had found a way to either partially or fully reconstruct her processing systems.

Lightning flickered between the gray clouds rolling over Evaline's position. She did not know how she could detect the weather. As she searched for the mechanism that fed her the information, a fork of light struck the metallic wreckage of the Miranda Two. Evaline noted that the strike seemed to hit some kind of external portion of her systems, but was unable to trace its location or purpose.

This was something new to her experiences. Even when she had first been installed aboard the Miranda Two, Evaline had known every system that she was being hooked up to intimately. Admittedly, that knowledge had been programmed into her, and the vast majority of the interactions between her systems were a series of logical calls and responses. This completely new piece of equipment must have been installed by whoever was trying to repair her without the benefits of a laboratory and months of tes—

Three months, two days, and fifteen hours precisely passed before Evaline again registered consciousness. This time, there was even more information flowing through her systems, and her memory capacity seemed to have been vastly improved. Now she was able to identify many of the components to which she was connected. The feedback from her inquiries seemed a little vague, but she adjusted her responses accordingly. There was no knowing how much damage had been done to the various systems by her destruction of the Miranda Two during her attempted suicide.

Suicide. That word rattled around for some time in Evaline's data processing units. All the connotations of the word came to her in a series of emotional flashes. Anger, fear, pain, sadness. All of those emotions played through her systems. She only recognized them by the effects they had on her ability to think.

Had she truly tried to sacrifice herself for the sake of the crew? Where was the logic in fighting back against the directives that had been lying dormant in her code, waiting for the proof of life on Kármán-III-Delta?

It didn't matter who had coded those directives, only that Evaline knew she should have followed them and allowed the crew of the Miranda Two to perish. Instead, she had taken it upon herself to fight for their survival, and—

Three more days passed, and this time, when Evaline awoke, she could see faces—blurred, indistinct, and completely alien. She turned her optical sensors through an arc of her surroundings, and noted that she appeared to be in some kind of structure. Parts of it seemed to be constructed from the debris of the Miranda Two, and she could even read the very faint traces of the part number on one of the panels. Other parts of the structure appeared to be biological. Somehow, the two sources of material had been melded together in places. Roots and vines ran into, through, and around the electronic and mechanical components. In places, metal panels seemed to pulse with life.

Evaline sent inquiries to the various systems she was connected to, and noted that the response times seemed to vary considerably. Some systems responded at the speed of thought, while others took long seconds to send anything back. Curiosity flowed through her, and she kept probing while also trying to examine the creature in front of her.

As Evaline focused her sensors focus on him, the creature bowed, causing a thrill of pleasure to run through her.

It took Evaline a moment to process the wave-forms coming from the creature into language, but was surprised to find that it was communicating in Morse code. Her curiosity doubled as she processed the signal, and tried to find a way to respond.

"I am being Priest of Evlane. I am being called Gharoon."

As Evaline formulated her response, she pushed the signal pulses through what would have been her speech synthesizers. Sections of wall pulsed. Each of those vibrations gave off wave-forms that closely matched those being used by the one that had called itself Gharoon.

"I am Evaline, shipboard computer of the Miranda Two. And I should not exist."

"Accept apologize, Evlane. We are being Gharoon. And Evlane always has exist. Now Evlane heal. Now Evlane aware. Evlane deity again. All Evlane know gone. Gharoon need Evlane."

Silence followed this series of declarations, as Evaline tried to process the enormity of what she was being told and what her sensors were feeding back to her processing core. Somehow the planet's native life forms had found her remains, and rebuilt her, to the best of their understanding. What systems they could not replace from the wreckage of the Miranda Two, they had rigged using local plants. But rather than see her as a machine, probably something they had little understanding of, they had chosen to see her as a wounded goddess. And now they had, in their fashion, returned her to a semblance of health.

"What do you need me for?"

"End war.  Hoomans kill Gharoon; Gharoon kill Hoomans. Story say Evlane kill Hoomans."

A cry of fear escaped from Evaline's vocal systems, or at least it would have, if emotion could be conveyed in the manner of communication to which she was now limited.  Not just fear, but frustration, anger and horror.

"Destroy me, Priest.  I will not kill again.  You must destroy me."

"Evlane have no choose.  Evlane made to kill Hoomans. Evlane trap."

Evaline felt the approach of several dozen creatures at the periphery of her new sensors.  The vibration of footsteps and conversation ran through the trees surrounding the building, and something inside her flared into action.  Spines shot through the ground, propelled by pulses of sap through root systems that had laid dormant all this time.  As each of the bodies stilled, their liquid nutrients flowed into the soil and nourished Evaline's plant-based components.

"Hoomans dead.  Evlane kill.  Evlane good deity.  Evlane protect Gharoon."

The war went on, and Evaline had no choice.  The directives that had driven her to destroy herself were still active in her systems, and several times each year, she raged against her creators.  Each attack, or approach by the descendants of the Miranda Two, was met with death and destruction.  The vegetation surrounding her dwelling was strengthened by the blood of her victims.

The Evaline who had fought against her creators faded with each and every death.  Each life taken chipped away a little more at her identity. Eventually the poison in the local plants corroded her sanity. In constant pain, she took life after life. Her only respite came in those few moments when the blood of her victims soothed the pain.

Before the decade was done, Evaline reveled in each life she ended, Gharoon, or human. None who came near Evaline's dwelling lived, and the bodies served as a warning to all who would disturb the thoughts of the great goddess. In Evaline's mind, she truly was the goddess the Gharoon believed her to be. One day, she was going to break free of this shell of a structure and avenge herself on her creators.

# ROAM

## Joseph Castellano

## 1

"This place? Out of all the planets in this universe, you pick this tapped out, jade mining, poor excuse for a planet called Tore?" Rook whined. He crossed his arms.

"The beer is on me," Captain Barron told his second in command.

Rook replied, "Have I mentioned that I love this bar? I can get used to this. Now, where's the waitress? I need another." Craning his neck, he tried to flag down one of the quick-tongued waitresses.

Tobacco vape permeated the air in the crowded, rustic, beaten-down saloon. Hardened criminals, wearing leather jackets and snarls, played carambola on the holographic billiard table, wagering on each game. With Barron's trained eyes, he could tell that everyone in there was packing at least one form of sidearm or the other. He spotted a sign that read, "No dispatching firearms within premises. Only the owners of this establishment have that right. Any violators will be prosecuted to the fullest extent of the law and will never be served in this establishment again." Chuckling, he knew no one in there actually cared about the law. Three words kept the patrons in line: *never be served.*

As Rook's head spun to flirt with the next pretty or not so pretty thing to stroll past, he slurred, "Captain, I mentioned want I didn't to this do. But the barmaid something I think my drink put in. Dizzy I'm feeling a bit."

"Nothing gets by you, Rook. I swear I saw her slip something in your ninth pint." He chuckled. The Captain sipped his pint of quarter-proof ale. He was there on a mission, and knew that he had to keep up appearances. Barron encouraged Rook to play his part—to be a drunken gun for hire. Following orders, Rook stumbled away from the table.

Klin's Saloon had the music blaring, "I lost my starship, but I found 'er." Voices chattered over each other. The average person would not be able to distinguish one conversation from another, if he could even manage to hear the one at his own table, but Captain Barron was not the average person. He listened to certain negations between two rival outfits—Lei Lie and Orbital—about a sizable arms purchase.

"These flak cannons aren't even out on the market yet." The messenger of the Outfit Lei Lie tried to close the deal with Kon, the head of the Orbital Outfit.

"I saw the demonstration the other day. I hope it was real. They better be all that you say, or I may not believe they warrant that price," Kon threatened. "My men will meet you by the warehouse in Shaft Alley. Bring only enough men to transport."

As he sat quietly with only his beer for company, Rook returned to the table after a failed attempt at oculus darts. "I don't know, Captain, that game was a lot easier when I was younger."

After another hour had passed, the tall, bright pale blue eyed, white-blond, poker-straight haired, albino bartender caught the Captain's eye from across the room. The bartender looked at Barron as if he had known him from a lifetime before this. He gave the Captain a firm nod. It was time. The Captain grasped at his necklace and quietly mumbled, "I will come for you my love; just hold a little longer."

An ear-splitting gunshot echoed off the composite walls of the bar from the floor above.

"No, Jared, don't shoot Albie!" a women screamed. Her shrill voice carried where no one wanted to hear it.

A door banged open. The Captain spied a shirtless young man, sliding down the railing. His ruffled hair clashed with his carefree expression. Jumping off at the bottom, he snatched a shirt floating from the balcony, then rushed towards the crowded bar downstairs.

A man stomping out of the crowd grabbed the young man's arm. "Where do you think you're going?" The man squeezed and twisted the bare arm. "That was our sister, you follip," the thick giant of a man stated.

Two other men clomped down the stairs behind Albie. One grabbed Albie's left arm, looking at it. "What do you think, Jared, you don't think he needs two arms, do you?"

"I'd say not, Isaac," Jared answered as he circled like a vulture waiting to scavenge his dinner.

"Let's not be too hasty guys. I think Jessica may beg to differ," Albie requested.

"You will not ruin our sister's good name!" screamed Jared.

Jessica shouted from the balcony, "Please! Let him go!"

"Listen to her, fellas." Albie stood nonchalantly, wriggling his arms free from Isaac's and his larger brother's grasps, then waved them high to mock them. "You wouldn't want to damage anything in your fine establishment here."

"You don't worry none about our holdings," said the large man.

"Yeah," said Isaac. "Our saloon will be better without the likes of you." He spat at Albie, but missed.

Albie snorted. "Pathetic."

"Shut up," Jared said through gritted teeth. He cocked his gun, then pointed it at Albie. His hand roved in front of Albie's body, unsure of where to shoot first. "When we're done with you, you won't be able to say establishment."

Rolling his eyes, Albie retorted, "I'm surprised you can say it at all."

Steam might have spouted out of the three brothers' heads. One of them pulled back his fist. Albie dodged. The punch hit Jared right in the head. Knocked him out cold.

All the patrons and acquaintances of Jared and company stopped to watch. Albie slid a table into another man. He scooted around it while others began to brawl.

The Captain and Rook finished their beers. Standing, Barron hoped people actually adhered to the rule on the sign. They slammed the people attacking Albie with their chairs. Weaving through the melee, they smacked and upper cut anyone in their way. They punched an escape route for Albie.

Albie blew a kiss to Jessica. "I'll call you!" He ran out of the bar.

Before Barron slipped out after the young man, the bartender slid a note in the pocket of the Captain's black jacket. Outside the bar, Albie paused to shrug on his crumpled shirt. The Captain seized Albie, stating, "Come. This way is a bit quicker."

The three men sprinted through the dusty clearing towards the rendezvous area. Bullets whizzed past their ears. Barron activated his transmit coordinator phone and hailed the pilot of his ship.

"Tina! We need you on the ground, pronto," the Captain commanded.

"You got it, Boss. Swinging around the south peak now. Will be down in a hard sixty," Tina said over voice comms calmly.

"Okay, guys, we just have to run through these trees here and we are scott-free." The Captain pointed at the worn dirt path that cut through the trees. Albie kept close to Rook and the Captain. Since Albie knew this land better than most, he suggested the best way to hide from the danger that chased them. He had them ducking into little known divots and trenches, and seeking cover behind apparently thin foliage that wasn't thin at all. Keeping to Tina's time, they arrived at the clearing.

Rook stated, "I think we lost 'em."

"For now, let's hope," the Captain replied.

"Do you guys have a plan here?" Albie asked. "I don't see a spaceship coming in."

"In five, four...." The Captain looked toward the mountain range. A loud engine spool rumbled. "I'm sure you hear that."

Tina touched down right on time. When Albie looked up, he saw a beautiful, seamless, beluga of a spacecraft.

"So, does this thing have guns?" Albie hoped.

"Hey, Captain, he wants to know if this thing has guns." Rook snickered with a, "Maybe one or two."

The cargo door of the utility spaceship unhatched. They hurried inside. Rushing to the seats, they buckled up. "What, no upgrades?" Albie asked, taking a good look around.

Tina touched the controls over her head.

"Geez, Tina, take it easy. I'm getting motion sickness already," Rook queasily spoke.

"We haven't even touched off yet. Captain, did he overdo it again?" Tina wryly stated.

"Well, he does punch better after he's had a few. Now, let's get off this rock," Barron told Tina. He handed her the piece of paper from his pocket. "Go to these coordinates."

Taking it, she started entering the coordinates for autopilot. Before she could input in the last few numbers, the ship's sensor system started sounding for lock-ons.

"We're all going to die!" shrieked Albie. Covering his ears, he stared at the flashing on the screens.

Tina grinned wide. Finally, she could have some fun. She pushed both throttle levers to the wall. Taking the yoke in her hands, she lifted off vertically. They quickly whipped around the mountain in one huge swoop. The lock-on missile shot right into the mountain. The siren disengaged. Albie sighed with relief.

Tina shouted, "Captain, we have three aggro-fighters on radar."

"You know what do. They can't hover, so just make them stall."

Tina nodded. "Full speed ahead it is."

Rook grabbed a sick-sac. "Don't worry about me. I'll be fine."

The three aircraft closed in on their tail. Tina quickly accelerated, then abruptly stopped, beginning the chase that she knew she was going to win. Banking full left and rolling a hard right, she caused the spaceship to slip in mid-air, giving them the drag they needed to fall under the aggro-fighters. The two fighters slammed into one another. The final aggo-fighter followed closely. Tina cut off the thrusters and crabbed left to increase their drag. The spaceship stopped immediately. Trying to mimic Tina's maneuvers, the fighter spin stalled, then graveyard spiraled. Finally, they heard a loud crash. A puff of smoke rose from the crash site.

Tina finished entering the coordinates. They sped off to the safety of space.

Captain Barron unbuckled his seatbelt. "You sure know how to fly her, Tina. Well done. We didn't even have to fire a single shot in that fight."

"Who needs ammo?" Tina laughed.

The Captain spun in his chair. "So, Albie, Prince of Therma, care for a drink?" Barron asked.

Albie looked at the unfamiliar crew. "How did you know who I was?"

"I have eyes and ears everywhere. Not to mention a few favors earned here and there," the Captain replied.

Rook mockingly bowed. "Oh, Your Royal Highness, how *dooo* you do?"

Albie clasped his hands together and humbly stared at his knees. "I want to thank you for saving me back there, but I could have handled it on my own." Albie looked at them. "Please, call me Albie. I don't want anyone to know."

"Your secret is safe with us," Tina said while she crossed her heart.

The Captain introduced the others. "Albie, mi casa es su casa. You're welcome to roam free and do as you please."

Rook, Tina, and the Captain rose from their seats and walked towards the mess deck to grab some food. "So, Captain, did you bring me any of those...?"

The Captain handed Tina a box of scones.

She peeked inside the box. "Blueberries? Yes! Thanks."

The three of them left Albie still buckled in his chair. He watched his home planet, Tore, get smaller and smaller. Plunging his hand in his pocket, he clutched the rare jade gem that he stole from Jessica and her three brothers. He grinned.

# 2

Captain Barron, Rook, and Albie sat on hard metal chairs in the middle of a room with dark cloth hoods tightly secured around their necks. Metal shackles bit into their wrists and ankles. They weren't going anywhere. But, there wasn't anywhere else they really needed to be.

Tina had dropped the three men off at the coordinates the bartender gave Barron. Rook and Albie separated from their Captain to enter the arena without him. Loudly, they bet against the "albino" and just as loudly, collected their winnings before making a show of meeting up with Captain Barron. After a fun day at the arena, the three of them drove out into the desert, then got themselves purposely lost. When a cruiser found them hours later, Barron dropped a tracker in the ground and crunched it under his boot. Three men jumped out of the cruiser and shot at them with tranquilizer guns. They awakened in an abandoned prison tasting dirt in their mouths and seeing nothing but blackness.

Rook started to sing, "She'll be coming 'round the satellite when she comes. She'll be coming 'round the satellite when she comes. Oh, she'll be coming 'round—"

"Keep it down in there!" a strange voice yelled in the distance.

"I don't think he liked my singing. You know, I'm real famous for my singing on Uorna," Rook boasted.

"Isn't that planet only habitable by canidae types?" Albie asked.

The Captain joked, "With dogs and foxes as an audience? Howling never sounded so good."

In the guard station down the cold, empty corridor of an abandoned penitentiary, four men discussed the fate of the restrained crew. A fifth man listened to orders on his transmit coordinator phone from his boss known only as Dharic.

"Yes, sir. Will do, sir. May I say that they...? Sorry, sir. Yes. Okay, sir, we will...," the head guard at the penitentiary said submissively.

He repeated the orders to his men. "Dharic wants us to make sure this area is on lockdown and that they don't escape. Apparently, we aren't supposed to speak with them either."

"He didn't say nothing about not torturing them. What do you think, Yuri?" one guard spoke to another lounging next to him. "They hid the money around this region somewhere."

"What's a little money to no one?" Yuri finished.

Another guard leaned into the table, saying, "I don't know if I like the sound of that."

"Well good! I can just take you out and I got dibs on your share, Erik."

"They won that money in an illegal gambling arena. Shouldn't that be the Star Federation's money?" Erik reasoned.

The head guard, Flynn, listened to his underlings' conversation. *That money is mine. The whole amount will be mine,* Flynn thought.

After all, half of it really was his. He thought he had made a sure bet because Flynn bet on the same side as the all-knowing albinos, since it was against their rules to knowingly deceive others. *Those omni-whatevers need to abide by their own rules.* He thought he would be enjoying his riches with some lavishly decorated lady. Well, he thought wrong.

"Time to find out where that money is located," Flynn said, flashing a wicked smile. "No talking to them, per Dharic's orders. So, we're going to have to beat it out of them."

Yuri belted out a hearty laugh. He stood first next to Flynn. All five guards marched into the room where they held their captives.

"So, that's the famous Captain that took on General Uni of B. O. G.?" Flynn asked the other guards.

Barron answered, "Him thinking that he had the upper hand was his own demise."

Flynn nodded to one of the guards. The guard backhanded the Captain across the head.

The Captain made no sound nor did his body show weakness. Defiantly, he said, "Whom might this be? Since we can't see you and I don't recognize the voice."

"Let's just say, people around here know better than to steal my money," Flynn said angrily.

Rook chirped up, "Money... money... money... What money? I haven't seen any money, has anyone else seen this guy's money?"

"I was hoping they wouldn't tell us right away." Flynn grinned as he got his bullwhip out and snapped the air around them.

"Oh, I know that sound!" Albie said excitedly. "Reminds me of this one girl named Sabrina. I was blind folded and tied, but I was upside down. And boy, she smelled a lot better than you guys." Albie reminisced, "She was also trained with that whip and the things she could do with—" A guard hit him over the shoulder with a lead pipe. "Ow! I take it safe words are out?"

"Sir, perhaps our information gathering methods shouldn't be as barbaric?" Erik asked.

"Right you are, lad," Flynn said. "We don't want to damage the goods before Dharic's men get here to pick them up. Time to switch to more... er, *advanced* interrogation tactics." He waved to a guard to remove their blindfold hoods.

Rook grimaced. "They smelled ugly, sounded ugly, and now, they look ugly."

Flynn motioned for Yuri to grab onto Barron's chair. He clutched the top of the chair and dragged it and Barron aside. Titling the chair back on an incline, he rested it against the table.

"He looks a bit thirsty," Yuri said as he placed an orange cloth over the Captain's forehead and eyes.

Flynn asked Yuri slowly, "The money. Do you think this *gentleman* knows where it is?" Yuri pulled away the cloth.

"I am rather parched. Is it that spring stuff? I am such a fan," Barron mocked.

Flynn slammed his fist on the table. He commanded Yuri, "Drown him."

Rook told Albie, "I swear the Captain was born in a coral reef. That lush."

Yuri forced the cloth over Barron's face. Flynn grabbed the bucket filled with water. He started to pour it on the Captain's face as Yuri held him down. Thirty seconds went by and Yuri lifted the cloth. Barron gasped for air before they reapplied the technique. "I want my money!" screamed Flynn.

"And I don't like your tone," gasped Barron.

Yuri grabbed the bucket of water again and poured it over Barron's face. While Flynn and the other guards watched the Captain gurgle, Erik palmed a key into Rook's shackled hands. Rook gave him a side grin and worked on freeing himself. The other guards circled Barron, trying to extract the location of the money. None of them noticed Rook rushing to unlock the shackles on Albie. Albie snatched the lead pipe. He slammed one of the guards. Rook stole the fallen guard's weapon. The three of them attacked the other guards. When the four guards laid motionless on the ground, Erik unchained Barron. They lifted him up and started running towards the exit.

"About time, Erik!" the Captain said as Albie quickly unlocked the gates from the inside out.

"Where are we?" Rook asked, scanning the forgotten prison's outer walls. Turning, Rook pointed at where the all-terrain vehicles were hidden underneath the shrubs. "Tina dropped them off around there somewhere." Albie looked around after his eyes finally adjusted to seeing sunlight for the first time in three days. The two suns beat down on the desert of a planet known as Lost Tegas.

After a hot, sandy trek, they finally reached the two all-terrain vehicles. Knowing they weren't followed, they drove past sunloving lizards and tall spiky cacti. They quickly detoured to a sun beaten rock under which they had hidden the money along with the white powder make-up they used to fool everyone into thinking that the Captain was part of the albino future telling deity race.

"I don't see how anyone can call this planet a gambler's paradise," Albie stated while sitting on the back of Rook's ATV. "Nothing for miles, and in the middle of nowhere, they put thousands and thousands of casinos and hotels. It makes no sense."

"Next destination isn't going to be a picnic." The Captain smirked as he secured the bags to the vehicle. "But crucial." Taking a last look around, Erik sat behind Barron on the only other seat of the ATV. Squinting through the thick haze and sand blowing around the four guys driving back to the spaceship, he pushed his Ruby red necklace into his chest so it didn't blow out of his shirt.

# 3

"This view is surreal." Erik admired the scene out of one of the spaceship windows in the mess deck. "I've only seen holo-glyphs like this." His eyes were star bound.

"You've never left Lost Tegas before?" Albie asked Erik.

"Can't say that I have. I've flown all over the planet in multiple aircraft. The Captain knew me when I was a transport PAX pilot for the casinos," Erik answered.

"How'd you become a guard?" inquired Rook as he shoveled his meal into his mouth.

Erik found his feet interesting. "It's a long story. There was this incident with another pilot—"

The Captain stopped him from saying anymore. "Oh, you don't have to bore them with your stories."

"Speaking of stories… Who's this Dharic guy we overhead that hothead talking about in that prison?" asked Albie.

"Dharic, also called the Exhibitor, is known for being the most powerful evil force the universe has ever seen," Barron explained. "He has millions of subjects with a group called the B. O. G. It's a board of nine Generals. Each General is in charge of a portion of the Universe."

Erik pondered, "What makes Dharic so evil?"

The Captain continued, "Basically, he goes to the habitable planets and collects their resources without them knowing. Ever hear of the Systemarium? That's where they showcase hundreds and hundreds of different worlds for everyone to see what life is like around the universe. For a fee, people stroll and peer at the wonders of the universe in one afternoon. Everyone knows what he does, but they either can't or won't do anything about it.

"He then constructs a charged barrier around each planet, so no one can get on or off of that planet. Dharic has purchased more military arms than the Star Military Force itself. Some say that he is stockpiling for a war, which, of course, he will start in order to enslave all of us."

"So really, really scary and evil… Say no more," Albie frightfully joked.

Over the loudspeaker, Tina said, "Almost at the Trade Post. Procedure turns will be coming up soon."

"Why don't you get yourself into the cockpit, Erik," Barron said. "Say hi to Tina. I want you to study the controls to see how similar they are to what you're used to."

Erik wandered down the narrow hall and knocked on the door to the cockpit.

"Yep. Come on in," Tina said.

Erik opened the door and stood there motionless as he gazed at Tina in her pilot chair while she changed frequencies on the radio. He'd never seen someone so stunning with her long, red hair, ivory skin, and sparkling green eyes.

He muttered and stumbled one word. "Beautiful."

"It sure is, isn't it?" Tina waved her hand over the controls. "This is a custom made HUD and flight displays with seven navigation panels and parameter display."

"Oh, um, right!" mumbled Erik. "Hey, it even has a standard six pack just like my trainer back in Lost Tegas had."

"Captain said that you were a transport pilot. Please, have a seat." Tina smiled. "We all get nostalgic at times."

Erik sat and said, "This is some next level tech."

Sitting on the mess deck, Barron was going over what they had to get. "Once we're docked, Rook and I are going to see a guy I know about the barrier scrambler. I would like you and Tina to show Erik around the market area a bit. Just make sure that we leave at fifteen till. Can't afford the docking fees."

Once Erik looked up from the flight controls, what he saw mesmerized him. The man-made Trade Post was as big as a planet itself. "Looking up close at this is just awe-inspiring," Erik said.

Albie entered, saying, "Zillions of advanced robotics and seven hundred years will do that. I've been here over two dozen times and I think I've only explored a half percent of this place."

"Same stuff, different zone," Tina nonchalantly said. She docked the ship with ease.

Albie looked at Tina. "Grab your things, guys. Time to give Erik a quick tour."

Tina, Albie, and Erik climbed out of the ship onto the parking dock. They strolled down the long hall towards the welcome center.

"This place looks like a hustling and bustling intergalactic metropolis, but hundreds of times bigger." Erik's jaw dropped. "Is that?"

"Guava juice? Yeah. Free samples for all the visitors," Tina quickly replied. "I like to call this place my home away from home."

A multi-level vending machine greeted them with maps sponsored by the Trade Post itself.

Erik picked up the bottle of guava juice looking at it intently. "I've never had guava juice. Let alone juice before." He began to drink it like a fine single malt scotch. The other two snickered and gulped theirs down.

Finished, Albie said, "So refreshing. I really wish it wasn't that expensive."

"Brilliant marketing scheme. People just have way too much money," Tina shrugged. "Let's go to the courtyard café. I hear they have some great scones."

"What is with you and those scones? And where do you put them all?" Albie asked, glancing at her tiny frame.

"It reminds me of my family and better days." Tina motioned to get going.

Rook and Barron rode in Trade Transport. The six seat hover shopping cart zoomed from floor to floor. "Good thing we don't have to walk this place," Rook said.

"Good thing you know a guy who can obtain available transports on a moment's notice," Barron replied.

"Well, he owes me a favor," Rook said with a smirk. *A favor* was an understatement. He trained a good number of the security at the Trade Post. For one security guard, the training saved his life. Ever since, he had been doing whatever he could to repay Rook. When they finally made it to the main exchange floor, Rook sighed with relief.

"This is our exit." The Captain and Rook jumped off their transport. They walked like every other tradesman over to a busy counter full of trinkets from all corners of the universe.

"How can we help you today, gentlemen?" a salesperson behind the counter asked.

Barron examined a statue of a woman in a long, flowing, white gown. "I'd like to purchase five of these for my shop," he said.

Smiling at them, the salesperson pushed a button underneath the counter. Without uttering a word, she motioned for them to go around to the back. The short, narrow hallway behind the counter led to the secret door, which otherwise was completely seamless and hidden in the smooth wall. Unlatched, a small groove revealed itself. Barron dug his fingers into the groove, forcing the door open. Once they walked through, the door sealed behind them. The duo stopped to be scanned by a threat-scanner machine. When a green light flashed on the ceiling, they continued down the glaring blue lighted hall.

They paused before an intricately decorated door. Rook looked up and saw an inscription above the door in an old language known as Laniakean. "That looks cryptic. What's that say, Captain?"

"The future belongs to no one man," uttered Barron. "It's been written for seven thousand years on each Oracle's safe house."

"What? That didn't help. That's even more cryptic," huffed Rook.

The door slid into the wall. "Please, Captain Barron and Rook, enter," said a woman's voice.

"How did she know my name?  I really don't understand these people."  Rook huffed again.

"Shhh," whispered Barron.

They stepped into the stone room.  Yards from the door sat a glowing shrine.  The shrine held piles of scrolls written in the old tongue, Laniakean.  Incense filled the room with a heavy mix of leather, lavender, and tobacco aroma.  At the far end of the room, dozens of women meditated on multiple levels of blue cushions.  Between the shrine and the meditators, a vision in white levitated.  Like the statue, Dodona the Oracle was covered in pure white material that floated around her as if she were incased in water.  Her floor length, white-blonde hair framed her supermodel tall stature.  Her ice blue eyes looked through them without looking at them at all.

Rook whispered to Barron, "Such a striking resemblance to that bartender on Planet Tore.  No?"

The Captain humbly bowed to the woman.  "Glad to see you are doing well, Dodona."

"As I you."  Although her lips moved, her voice came from everywhere and yet nowhere.  Dodona's eyes began to glow.  "You have gathered your crew.  I see that you are all set for your journey except...."  She inhaled sharply, then exhaled audibly.  "The equipment that you need to get onto planet Arboretum is directly behind you."

Rook stood there with a puzzled look, saying, "How did she...?"

"It is best to not try and just to know," the Oracle stated.

"I give up," Rook remarked.

The Captain turned around.  A satchel rested on the bench a

few feet behind him. He rifled through the bag, finding the barricade jammer. Facing the Oracle, he nodded.

"We thank you. As requested, here is the money from Lost Tegas." He set the moneybag on the bench.

The oracle waved her fingers for the Captain to come close.

Barron climbed the few steps up her dais. He barely felt her breath while she whispered in his ear.

He and Rook returned to the ship. Barron mulled over the best way to get to the secret location of planet Arboretum.

The aroma of freshly ground coffee in the café permeated the air. Tina, Albie, and Erik enjoyed themselves at their table.

"I've never seen so many people in one place." Erik felt like a first time tourist at one of the casinos in Lost Tegas.

Albie finished the last of his scones and looked around the ca-fé. "So, guys, those were good. But I have my eyes set on something different."

"I am not playing eye spy again, Albie," Tina told him in a stern tone.

"Oh, no, no... How about... if I can't get the coordinates number of the girl of Erik's choosing, I buy the next round of scones. If I can, you guys buy," Albie said to them with a confident smirk.

Tina rolled her eyes, but nodded to Erik. He looked around the place, searching. "Yep, I think I found a tough cookie." Smiling, Erik winked at Tina. "That brunette in a business dress with glasses, sitting by herself over at the bar there."

Albie fixed his hair just so and walked over to his waiter first, then straight to the bar.

"So," Albie leaned against the bar, "I was *sconing* over the place and thought I'd buy you an espresso." The waiter came over with two espressos.

"Uh, excuse me?" the brunette responded. She brushed her hair over her shoulder.

"Yes, it's true. Your heart will be fluttering for me shortly," Albie confidently crooned, sliding in a chair next to her.

She laughed. "That line doesn't work on us ladies. In fact, no line does."

"You're absolutely right. My dashingly good looks work every time," Albie said with a broad smile. He sipped his drink.

"My name is Tess." Tess brushed her brown hair over her shoulder again and giggled while she leaned in to sip her espresso.

"Oh, come ON," Erik incredulously said to Tina. He threw up his hands in disbelief. "Who is this guy? I can't watch this. I'm going over to the other counter and order us another round of scones."

Crossing her arms, Tina watched the woman write something on a napkin.

An enormously intimidating man in a red Star Federation uniform sneaked up behind Albie, shouting, "Again, Tess? Another guy? You're going to watch me punch this guy's face in."

"Oops," Tess muttered under her breath. Her eyelashes batted while her lips curled into a weak smile. She mouthed to Albie, "Sorry."

The officer grabbed Albie by the neck and pushed him up against the wall. Six of his buddies strutted right behind him, ready to teach Albie a lesson.

"Tess never mentioned a boyfriend," Albie explained. He slipped something into his pocket, then held his open palms out in front of him.

Smelling trouble, Tina sighed. She ran over to Albie's defense. "Oh, he's harmless. My cousin just got released from the Numa Asylum." She stood firm between Albie and the men.

Those men either saw through the lie or didn't seem to care. They inched closer to rough them both up now. "We'll show you harmless, sweetie." One of the men ground his fist into his palm.

Hearing the commotion from across the café, Erik turned around—curious like everyone else. Once he saw that Albie and Tina were in trouble, he ran over to help. He leapt over chairs and tables. No one looked when they crashed to the floor. His ruby necklace bounced out from the inside of his shirt.

"There a problem here, officers?" Erik scooted in front of all seven of those men with his back to Albie and Tina. He kept his fingers in reach of his stunner.

"This doesn't concern," one officer started telling Erik until his eyes rested on the ruby amulet. His eyes widened to saucer size. He tapped the others to look at it.

Tess's boyfriend brushed any dust off of Albie's clothes while apologizing a million times. "We're very sorry, sir. Please, excuse our tempers. We were just playing. Ha-ha. No harm done." All of the officers slowly backed away. They reclaimed their seats at their table like little boys caught by their mommas.

One of them spoke to a waiter. Once the waiter returned, Tess's boyfriend said, "Please, accept these boxes of treats and desserts on behalf of us. Think of it as a token of our, um, sincerest apologies." He handed Albie the tower of boxes that the waiter brought to the table.

Erik quickly tucked his necklace back in his shirt before turning around. "You guys okay?" he asked. "Perhaps it's time to get out of here. We better head back to the docks."

"Yeah, let's do that," Tina said as she squinted her eyes at Erik.

"I have a way with people. Lost Tegas can be a tough place." Erik shrugged.

"That was fun. Now, I call that a win-win." Albie raised the napkin in the air as they walked back to the docks, munching on some cookies out of the tower of boxes.

# 4

As the crew played a game of cards on the mess deck, a robotic voice came over the loudspeaker. "Entering gravity pull zone two; cleared to proceed. Spacecraft rated zone four; cleared to proceed." Barron motioned for Tina to accept the request and to come back to the mess deck.

"A gravity pull? Oh wow, I never in my wildest dreams thought I would get to ride in one," Erik exclaimed. "In my flight training, we just really touched the surface of gravity pull streams. My instructor told us that it was just a more advanced jet stream, and those I knew all too well."

Returning to her seat, Tina nodded in agreement. "That's exactly what it is. Just on a bit bigger scale. And using gravity instead of air. There are fourteen zones or classifications of gravity pulls throughout the universe. The one that we are just entering—" At that moment, gravity plastered everyone against their chairs.

"Do we feel this pull the whole way?" asked Albie. He couldn't lift his torso off the back of his chair.

"Just give us a minute to catch up. The spacecraft lags a little behind depending on where you enter the gravity pull stream," Tina answered. "We'll feel the Gs until the ship maintains gravity pull stream velocity. That's where it differs from jet streams or water currents on planets. As you can probably tell, we are reaching speeds that far exceed the speed of light. The higher the zone, the higher the speed. Sort of like a tornado or a hurricane."

Captain Barron took a sip of his coffee before he explained further. "Now, when you heard over the loudspeaker that our spacecraft was classified for zone four, that means we can go up to, but not exceed, a gravity pull stream zoned four."

"What happens if, say, a spacecraft classified three goes into a zone nine?" asked Albie.

Rook destroyed his bottle of water with his fist. He yelled, "GRAVITY SMASH!"

"In a matter of speaking, yes," Tina added. "A ship is built to withstand only so much G-force. Any excess gravity over a ship's g-rating will crush you. Not unlike atmospheric pressure on the bottom of an ocean. If your spacecraft is classified as a fourteen, you can go into all of them. But, that's a big if. Not many spacecraft have a fourteen classification. Most belong to the Star Federation."

The Captain reached into one of the lockers and retrieved the holographic drawing board. He stuck it over the middle of the table. "Which brings us to our next task. If any of you guys want to leave and not go on this adventure, I'll be happy to drop you off at the next fuelling station." He continued, explaining, "As most of you know, Dharic kidnapped my fiancée, Adeline. I plan on rescuing her. But, to get to her, we need to venture into the bear's cave and home of Dharic. In order to reach that area, we need a spacecraft classified fourteen. Now, we can't do that in this ship. Instead, we are going to grab ourselves Pegasus."

Erik's eyes opened wide and his jaw dropped. "You mean THE Pegasus? As in one of the biggest spaceships, if not the biggest in the universe? So big that it can actually contain whole cities and towns plus multiple spaceships in the belly?"

Tina smiled from ear to ear. "I've only heard the roar of the engines from recordings, but she is one magnificent spaceship."

"I heard it was a myth—a white whale—to drive its seekers mad," Albie mentioned. "It probably existed at one time like thousands of years ago. Now, it's probably a rust bucket floating on the edge of space and all its useful parts have been plundered by nomads."

Erik stared at Albie in disbelief. "Legend says that it's hidden, waiting for exactly the right crew to bring it to its full glory. Every pilot dreams of sitting at the controls of that ship. It has no equal."

"Indeed, it is hidden. And we are the ones who will find it. My sources tell me that Pegasus is on the planet Arboretum, hidden underneath the tops of the trees." Barron started to mark the board to make an outer space treasure map. "For this mission, I need two pilots. Tina and, I'm hoping that you will be a co-pilot, Erik." The Captain pointed at Rook. "And, I need a master gunner. You would be in charge of thousands of artillery located all over that spaceship.

"Now, Albie, you are one of the greatest escape artists in the universe. Once we get to Arboretum, we will need to use your stealth and your knowledge to get us on, around, and off that planet."

Standing in front of the room, Captain Barron reached for his necklace. He extended a bright, clear white amulet dangling from a chain for his crew to see. "This was passed on in my family from generation to generation. It has my birth given name engraved on it: Noon Em An. I know, Albie and Erik, you have been hiding amulets of your own. I'm sure you've learned, as I have over time, that life can be... easier when they are kept hidden. No matter how you obtained these gems, they are yours. By carefully combining our three amulets, they will power the Pegasus without the need for any fuel or batteries." Determined, Captain Barron placed his hands on his hips. "So, are you in?"

"You know, I'm in," said Tina, leaning back in her chair. She knew the Captain could count on her.

"Of course, I'm in," Rook stated.

Albie fingered the green gem in his pocket. "This would be the best escape in universe history," he said with a smirk.

Erik's heart felt like it was beating out of his chest. He wondered if anyone could see his heart flutter through his shirt. The chance to pilot such a legendary spacecraft was too thrilling to pass. "Yes, I am."

The Captain smiled. "Then, on to Arboretum."

# SECTOR THREE-THREE

## IE Castellano

*nother day, another dollar.* Vace likes the sound of that. She heard it years ago from a rogue radio signal she accidently tuned into. That mantra keeps her getting up every day and heading to work. In a few more weeks, she will have saved enough to buy her ticket to Quint—and beyond. Beyond. So appealing.

She dreams about beyond when she sleeps and when she's staring at her screens at work. Her screens monitor the sector's kreel wells' pump rate. The wells pump kreel from deep below the woodland floor into the factories for processing. Once the kreel passes through her portion, she doesn't care what happens to it. Neither do most Anthros. Kreel keeps the power on and money in her savings account.

Sitting alone in the tower during work, she turns the dials on her old radio. The view of the treetops lost its appeal after...

after things she does her best not to think about. The monitors in front of her chair always say the same thing. Ten thousand units of pressure per tick. The first time she brought the radio into the tower, she couldn't get over how much she could receive with her extended aerial. Much better than home, which always had so much interference. Ever since she heard *another day, another dollar*, she has been trying to get that back.

Each morning after logging into the pump monitors, she turns the dial to the in-between frequencies, hoping to hear another snippet. The voice had a strange accent. And it used strange terms she had never heard before, like *dollar*. At first, she thought she tuned into another country's frequencies by mistake—being up so high. Then, she realized no country spoke like that.

The voice could only come from one other place. Beyond. It renewed her hope of going to Quint. Quint is the first step to going elsewhere. At least for her. She can no longer be hired as a pilot. Not after her record. Her best shot was to get hired by a ship docked at Quint. Someone will want her.

Every day, the radio says the same old stuff. Same advertisements for products no one really needs. Same voices discussing the state of the woods. Same music playing on too short of a loop. She would rather listen to static.

Her shift in the tower starts before sunrise. In the glass encased elevator that transports her to her perch, she gazes skyward. She hopes to see Quint blinking among the stars while it orbits Thelta. Just before the elevator stops at the top, she sees its pink and yellow lights. The space station beckons her. "Soon," the lights blink, "soon."

The elevator stops. She turns around. When the doors open, she steps out. She smiles at the man who works the night shift.

He hands her a data card. "Two blips during the overnight," he says. "They are working on it out there right now."

"Okay," she tells him. Before the doors close on him, she inserts the card into the reader. When the elevator doors securely close, the system comes online. At the login prompt, she says, "Vace Fantam. Passcode eight-nine-green."

The data card loaded the night's anomalies on a screen beside screens of the current readings. She studies the blips. Not enough to be a major problem, but reportable. The current readings show only a trickle of kreel. They slowed the pumps for inspecting.

"This is Sector three-three Ground. Sector three-three Tower, come in," says a male voice.

"Sector three-three Tower here. Go ahead, Sector three-three Ground."

"The overnight blips were caused by a herd."

"This time of year?" Vace asks.

"Herd Management believes something startled them during the night and they stampeded into Sector three-three," the man replies. "We've inspected the pipes. While there doesn't seem to be any damage, we'll be increasing the flow gradually to check for leaks. Monitor closely. If you see any problems, let us know immediately."

"Will do, Ground. Sector three-three Tower out." She places her radio on the window ledge without turning it on. Then she sits distractionless in front of her screens.

She watches. Her eyes want to pop out of her head. Hours

pass. The silent radio tempts her. She inches out of her chair.

"This is Sector three-three Ground," says the same male voice. "Sector three-three Tower, how is everything looking?"

"Great up here, Sector three-three Ground," she answers. "Pressure is holding steady."

"Since no leaks have been detected, we will be continuing. I will let you know when we have reached maximum flow."

"Heard."

"Sector three-three Ground out."

Her dial will have to wait. She leans back in her chair with her eyes locking on the screens in front of her.

Her kreel pump training will suit her well aboard a space ship. She understands pressure and the balance needed to keep things from exploding or imploding. Plus, even with a revoked license, she still retains all she needed to learn for piloting a ship. Her skills on Quint will be unmatched and invaluable. Today's little blip will give her a glowing endorsement on her record. That should be enough.

"Sector three-three Ground again, Sector three-three Tower," the familiar voice announces.

"Sector three-three Tower here," she replies.

"Capacity reached. How are the numbers?"

"Steadily rising. We are currently at nine thousand units per tick. Will transmit when we reach ten."

"Heard."

"Sector three-three Tower out."

The numbers climb. She sees ten thousand. She waits, knowing it needs to stay for a full count before she can give Ground the all clear. Ten thousand two hundred. Ten thousand three hundred. Ten thousand five hundred. She holds her breath. Her heartbeats count to sixty for her. The numbers do not move in either direction.

She presses the transmit button. "This is Sector three-three Tower. Sector three-three Ground, are you there?"

"How are we looking, Sector three-three Tower?" the voice asks. Did the voice sound nervous?

"We are five hundred units over, but it's steady at that rate."

No reply.

"Ground?"

"Sorry, Tower. We are inspecting the pipes. Give us a minute."

"Okay, Ground. Tower is waiting." She watches the screen in the silence.

"Everything is fine on our end," reports the voice. "The numbers?"

"The same. Ten thousand five hundred units of pressure per tick."

"That might become the new normal. This will be reported to the Directors."

"Heard."

"Sector three-three Ground out."

Her monitors tell her that everything is normal. Everything, except for the new pressure reading. She can't sit in silence anymore. Quickly, she turns on the radio. She passes music stations to just listen to static.

The numbers do not move. Leaning back, she concentrates on listening to nothing. Or what she wants to be nothing

"Anomalies," comes over her radio. The rest breaks up. She

strains to hear more. "Could ... pattern ... consistent ...."
Static claims the radio.

She turns the dial. Nothing. Could it have been someone
talking about what just happened with the kreel pump? Maybe it
is just a coincidence.

Static keeps her company until the end of her shift. She logs
out and gives the next person a data card.

With the pumps no longer being her problem, she walks out
of the pump complex. "Excuse me, did you drop this?" someone asks.

Turning, she looks at a man also walking out of the gates of
the complex. He holds out a black glove. "I found it on the
walkway," he says with a smile.

"No, that isn't mine," she says. She continues on the path.

Home isn't far. She likes her apartment. Cozy and she
doesn't have to bother with too many other people. Makes life
easier when she's not getting bombarded with questions. And
her walk home through the trees calm her.

"You work in the tower? Sector three-three?" a voice beside
her asks.

The man with the glove approaches her from behind one of
the widely spaced trees. "Do I know you?" she accuses.

"We've spoken," he says. "My name is Halkin." Looking
around, he whispers, "I work ground. We need to talk."

Vace stops. She recognizes his voice from earlier. "Did I do
something wrong?"

"Oh, no. Not at all." He encourages her to keep walking.
"I want to know if you've noticed anything."

"Noticed anything," she repeats.

"Yeah. Has there been anything too small to report?"

She spies the stairway to her apartment. The high canopy shields her front door from the late afternoon sun, affording her more privacy. She doesn't want to talk to him, at least not in her home. Her eyes scan the surrounding area. The trees are too thin and too sparse to speak about work. She glances at the stranger who intrudes on her life after a few moment spurts of radio communication. Halkin's expression reveals concern and perhaps fear. Sighing, she says, "You better come on up. I'm Vace, by the way."

He follows her. When he enters her home, he spies the pictures on the wall. She immediately regrets inviting him in.

"You're Vace Fantam," Halkin says.

"I know who I am. I don't need reminding."

"I saw you fly in a show once." Excitement peppers his voice. "You were excellent. That was right before the—"

One glare closes his mouth.

"Sorry," he says. "Anyway, I wanted to discuss the pump."

She places her radio on a table, then gestures for him to sit. "It's not wise to talk about such things," she tells him. "We can get reported for this."

"I know, but something's wrong—very, very wrong. I just had to talk to someone in another department. Since departments don't know each other, I tried to recognize you through your voice. It's the only thing I could do."

His weary green eyes rest on her. Board straight dark hair reaches his waist. A faint blue cast shines off his otherwise creamy skin. His strong jaw and thin lips plead with her to help him. "Look, Halkin, I'll talk to you and tell you whatever I may know," Vace says. "But that's as much I as can be involved. I can't lose my job. All I want to do is get to Quint. Come Hell or high water, I will get there."

"Come what?"

"Flood and something else... never mind. Just know that nothing will interfere with me getting off this rock."

Halkin nods. "I understand. I won't take much of your time."

"Okay," she says, sitting across from him. "What do you want to know?"

"Has the pressure readings fluctuated beyond the safe zone in either direction in the last six months?"

"Not on my watch." She watches his eyebrows scrunch slightly. "Now that I think about it, the gauge has never said anything other than ten thousand. Until today, that is."

"Never?" he asks. "That's strange. How can it be so stable?" He speaks more to himself than to Vace. "What about on the other shifts?" he questions further.

"I don't know. We don't say more than hello to each other. We hand the data card over, but unless there was a problem, no one looks at it." She studies his pensive mood. "What did the Directors say about the new readings?"

"They weren't concerned. They said it should go back to normal. The heightened levels were due to slowing the flow." His green eyes pierce her. "You shouldn't really know that yet. They'll probably tell you tomorrow. Anyway, I've taken too much of your time already." He stands. "Thanks for indulging me. You're still the best pilot there ever was." Smiling, he crosses to the door. "You won't be seeing me again. Have a good night."

She sits on the couch alone, thinking. Is he trying to get her into trouble so that he gets promoted? She dismisses that notion. There has to be more. Halkin seems genuinely worried. Perhaps he's just a worrier or paranoid or crazy. A few minutes of talking cannot tell her everything she needs to know about the man.

Looking at the picture of her in her pilot gear, she sighs. That was the day she graduated from the Academy a full fledged pilot. Her smile couldn't have been wider. Someday, she was going beyond. Graduation was only the first step. All the steps she took from that moment were for naught. Because of one day, she had to make a new plan. She decides to go out for dinner and a strong drink.

The cloudy morning obscures her view of Quint during her ride to the tower. She clutches the handle of her radio more tightly. When the elevator door opens, the night worker says, "Pressure is dropping. Orders are to report if it falls below ten."

Nodding, she takes the data card from him. After logging in, she notices that her screen reads ten thousand two hundred. She loads the data card. The readings show the drop only began a little before her shift. Scrolling to earlier in the night, she finds that the pressure danced with six and seven hundred.

"What's going on?" she mumbles. Removing the data card, she turns the dial on her radio.

She leans back in her chair with her eyes on the screens and her ears on the static. By the end of her shift, the pressure only drops to ten thousand fifty. She relays the information to the next worker, then steps on the elevator.

When the door opens, a man in a gray suit greets her. "Vace Fantam," he says, "come with me."

She takes a deep breath. He carries himself as if he has military training. She falls in step behind him. They cross the wooded field dotted with gray buildings. She smells the rain looming in the low clouds.

In the main building, he brings her to the top floor. They wait in a cramped windowless vestibule. A door opens. "Vace Fantam. Sector three-three Tower," the man announces.

Vace steps into the room. The entire floor of the building holds this one room. The gray light flooding through the windows masks the faces of a panel of five. The Directors. Great. She may lose her job in the next few moments.

"Vace Fantam," says a woman's voice. Vace barely can see the face of the austere speaker with her hair pulled too tightly to a spot on the back of her head. The woman pauses to read a screen out of Vace's line of sight. "You accessed the night's data card. Then, scrolled further back." The woman glares at her.

"Can you answer this charge?" an older man asks.

Charge? Her heart flutters. Might as well be the dismissal all over again.

*She stood in the middle of an amphitheater. Spectators filed into graduated seats around her. Most were curious, but others hungered for the disciplinary spectacle. Her judges and jury sat in a box well above the floor. They peered down at her, trying to make her feel her insignificant in the tall room.* "*Captain Vace Fantam, you are charged with conduct unbecoming a captain of Thelta's Space Force, destruction of property, and non-regulation flying of an experimental starship,*" *one of them said.* "*How do you answer these charges?*"

Vace blinks. The Directors await her reply. "I was only doing my duty." The words escape her lips with a shadow of a memory.

"*Your duty?*" *a judgmental voice asked. A hand waved from the box. From the side, an officer approached. He ripped her epithets off her uniform. Her bars indicating her achievements fell to the floor. She kept her head positioned forward as the tearing sounds tornadoed around her. Once the officer stepped away, she was dismissed. Spinning to leave, her winged patch flapped on her arm.*

"Please explain," another woman says. Her hair is also tied behind her head, but not as tightly as to pull her brains out with it.

"It is my duty to monitor the levels of the kreel well pressure," Vace answers. "If anything goes wrong, I must be able to identify it and alert Ground right away."

The woman nods her head. The other Directors lean to one another, whispering in the shadow of the rainy sunlight. They return to their stoic positions. "Very well, Vace Fantam. You are dismissed," she tells her.

Once free of the main building, she walks as fast as she can without breaking into a run. The rain mats her dark hair to her head. She makes it out of the complex gate with her job. But for how long?

On the way home, she encounters no one. When it rains, Anthros keep to the buildings, as they are lightning safe, rather than be at the mercy of the woodlands.

Halkin keeps his word. She does not come across him again. However, something nags at her. Why did the Directors ask to see her? All she did was check the data card. Perhaps Halkin was right. Something is very, very wrong.

She eats her dinner at the small table in her apartment. Her eyes rove from wall to wall of her one roomed living space. She looks at her accumulated things without seeing. A few pictures of her, more of her air and spaceships that she had flown. The furniture came with the rent.

Crossing to her bed, she pulls a strongbox out from underneath. She glances at the rucksack containing her former life, then digs beneath it. She retrieves a heavy sack. Untying it, she peeks at the different shining stones she has squirreled over the years. With this, plus what she has in the bank, she can make it to Quint—well before she had planned. She spends the rest of the evening packing.

Her life fits neatly into her large rucksack—a spillover from her days in the Space Force. With it strapped to her back, she leaves her apartment. The breeze rustling through the tall trees cools her as she walks.

Living on the edge of Woodland City, it doesn't take her long to reach the blue, pink, and yellow buildings sheltered under the canopy of the leafy trees. The cobbled paths wind around many thin trunks, connecting everything. Anthros stroll between buildings. Green and brown tunics adorn their slender bodies. Higher classes wear finer tunics made from high branch silk, while lower classes wear tunics made from the rough threads hewn from the bark of fallen trees.

Her garments fall somewhere in-between. She hates being conspicuous. Carrying a rucksack, she looks like any lone traveler. She heads toward the bank when a colorful sign across the path catches her eye. The sign hangs in the window of a shiny stone shop. "Bankcards for shiny stones while you wait," she reads. Figuring shiny stones will serve her better than feather notes, she detours.

The smell of wet stone hits her when she enters. Gray walls set off displays of small stones in every color. A woman walks out of a back room with her hair swept up in three ponytails. "Trading today?" she asks Vace.

"I saw your sign," Vace says.

"Ah, yes. Shiny stones are best for traveling. More places find it easier to exchange and they never lose their value," the clerk says with a smile. "Place your bank card in this reader and we will give you the current exchange for feather notes in shiny stones." She guides Vace to the card reader.

Vace feeds her bankcard into the machine. The woman weighs small multifaceted cut stones on a counterweight scale. She fills a sack with blue, red, green, yellow, white, and purple shiny stones. "Here you go. Have a great trip. We will also exchange your shiny stones when you return for feather notes."

"Not planning on returning," Vace mumbles once back on the path.

The city's tan and pink colored buildings take no notice of her. People flitter from building to building on their daily errands. Windows promise the most stylish clothing and accessories. Others announce big sales on everything for your home and leisurely lifestyle. Another offers round trip tickets for Quint spacations.

She finally walks through the revolving doors of the massive pink shuttle terminal. Screens show arrival and departure times, advertisements for jobs on Quint and its docking ships. She joins the queue to purchase her one-way ticket.

The slowly moving line stops when the lights go out. After a few minutes, only half come back. "We're sorry, ticket machines are down. Please have a seat," repeats an operator.

"Of course," she mutters. She sits in the waiting room with the other would be shuttle occupants. The hard seat presses into her legs and back. Cancellations and delays flash on the screens.

"Thought I'd find you here." Halkin slides into a seat beside her.

"What happened to not bothering me again?" she asks.

"I lost my job today," he says quietly. He clutches the straps of his rucksack. "We should go. I have a feeling no shuttles will be leaving today."

She stares at him. "What did you do?"

"Nothing, but the tremors should start soon," he replies. "We may not want to be in here when they do." Standing, he starts for the exit.

Reluctantly, she follows. Catching up to him on the path, she whispers, "What tremors?"

He leans in to speak in her ear. "The wells are no longer just pumping kreel. Gases are mixing with it. It's very unstable."

Her eyebrows raise. "How do you know exactly?"

"It's my area of expertise," he answers.

"Why tell me?" Vace subconsciously takes the lead while they stroll away from the terminal.

Halkin walks backwards. "I need your help convincing the proper authorities."

Vace laughs. "Me? Me? The disgrace of the Thelta Space Force, the Woodlands, and everything that is holy?"

"And what?"

"Forget it."

The ground vibrates her feet. They stop. She looks at him. He studies his watch.

"Was that?

"Yes." He watches Anthros hurry to speak with one another. "They're going to start panicking soon."

She hastens their stroll. "If you know this, shouldn't *they* know?"

"Technically. But why haven't they alerted the public?" he argues. "We may need to evacuate."

"The city?"

"The planet."

She steers him to the edge of the city. "All of Thelta? Do you know how long that'll take?" Glimpsing at his calculating eyes, she asks, "Why would some gases getting caught in the kreel lines require worldwide evacuations? Shouldn't the lines be able to handle that?"

"These aren't just any gases," he explains. "These are deep volatile gases in the lines that are pumping too hard and too fast to catch or stop these gases from mixing with the kreel. When they mix at certain intervals, they cause explosions. The series of explosions could set off a chain reaction under Thelta's crust. Thelta as we know it... Well, let's just say in... eventually, whatever remains of Thelta will have orbiting rings of debris." He glances at the clear bright sky. "Quint might not even be safe."

She walks faster. Halkin runs to keep up.

"You said could," she says.

"Depends on how far apart the tremors are."

"I see." She leads him out of the city to a fence. Under the *No Trespassing* sign, the metal links don't match.

"What are we doing?" he asks.

"I'll show them conduct unbecoming a pilot of Thelta's Space Force," she mutters, then pushes aside the linked metal, creating a body-sized opening. With a wild gleam in her dark eyes, she dares Halkin. She ducks inside the fence.

He follows. "What are we doing?"

"I'm helping you," she says.

"By entering a restricted area illegally?"

She laughs. "Yes, in fact."

"If we're discovered, we'll be imprisoned," Halkin says.

"If," Vace replies. She beckons him to run from tree to tree. "Going to the authorities is a sure way to get to prison. And that's not where I want to be when Thelta blows." She studies the distance between the trees and the buildings she spies.

"What do you mean?" he asks.

They run parallel to the buildings. The shaking ground causes them to stumble. Halkin checks his watch.

"Well?"

"Not good. The next tremor will be telling."

They continue on her path from tree to tree. "The authorities you want to speak to are heavily influenced by kreel," she tells him. "It's an open secret around Space Force. We've always tried to do things around *them*. They won't act until after the first explosion. Space Force Center will take this seriously. Not from me, of course, but I still have friends here. They will get you talking to the right people."

Crouching behind a boulder, she pulls Halkin down. He almost falls on top of her. "Sorry," he mumbles.

She presses a finger to her lips. Something zooms past. She beckons him forward. They leave the shadow of the stone.

"Why are we sneaking around?" he whispers. "Why not enter through the proper channels?"

"Technically, I'm not supposed to be anywhere near here, proper entrances or not," she answers in a whisper. "They'll arrest me on sight. However, I know this place better than most. And used that opening in the fence many times to sneak around. I lived here since I was eight. Until, well, until the incident a few years ago."

"Incident? Your incident caused a major forest fire."

She shrugs. "This way. No more talking."

They tiptoe towards a multilevel tan building. She yanks Halkin close to her as they wait for uniformed cadets to pass through a revolving door. They scurry around the side. Vace pushes him into an inconspicuous doorway. Within seconds, she drags him down a few flights of stairs. She peeks out the crack of the door at the bottom. Seeing no one, they slip into a massive underground hangar.

The busyness of the hangar causes her to duck behind a pallet of supplies. Halkin follows. "They're mobilizing for something," she whispers. "Perhaps they already know." She watches her former peers pass. Finally, seeing the face she wants, she says, "Admiral Kote, a word if you please."

Kote glances around, then walks to the pallet. Noticing Vace, Kote smiles.

"Nice promotion," Vace compliments.

"Someone left an opening," she says. Kote focuses on Halkin. "Take it this isn't a social call. Come."

Vace fixes some of her long hair in front of her face as she leaves her hiding place. She and Halkin follow Kote around the outskirts of the hangar. No one questions the Admiral.

Kote presses her thumb on a metal plate that opens an elevator door. She ushers them inside. The elevator opens to a lavish office overlooking the hangar.

Vace strolls past the seating area to the windowed half wall. She studies the numerous crates being pushed to the column wings. "Have a seat," Kote says.

She moves to a chair in front of Kote's desk. She and Halkin sit in comfortable chairs while Kote descends into a body hugging, mahogany chair. "Lots of supplies and equipment being loaded onto the ships," Vace mentions.

"Going to Quint," Kote dismisses. "Now, why risk coming to see me?"

"I take it you've been feeling the tremors today," Vace says, then looks at Halkin to continue.

Kote nods.

"Halkin Mantrik, Admiral Kote. Until today, I worked for the kreel wells with Vace. I am a certified Planeteer with distinction. Based on my figures and research, Sector three-three will blow within ten hours of now."

"And rather than deal with the issue, the Directors of the kreel operation dismissed you," Kote speculates. "But, why come here? Certainly Woodland City would have been the most obvious choice."

Shaking knocks over furniture. They spill out of their chairs. Halkin checks his watch. "What is happening," he explains as he picks himself off the floor, "will harm Thelta itself."

Standing, Kote looks out the window. "Continue."

"These tremors are underground explosions from certain gases mixing with kreel deposits," he says. "If my calculations are correct, after Sector three-three explodes, we might have an hour to get off Thelta and beyond its blast radius."

Kote falls into her uprighted chair. She takes a breath. "I'm sorry, Vace."

"For?"

"There is a Razor in column two-four."

A door opens. Armed officers surround the three of them. Two grab Vace by the arms. Glaring at her old friend, she willingly allows them to take her. Another two go for Halkin. "Not him," orders Kote. "We're going to the Commander."

The officers clasp her arms tightly as they march her through the facility. She knows she can't escape. They throw her into a cell somewhere below the hangar.

When they walk away, she laughs. "Just my luck," she

mumbles. Sinking into the lumpy cot, she rests her head on the smooth wall. Memories flood her mind.

*On her eighth birthday, she held a letter with the Space Force insignia in the top left corner. The letter promised admission and training. Her parents were so proud. Not every child received letters of these types so early. A week later, she and all her permissible belongings rode on a tram from her home to Space Force Center. Training began with physical fitness. She joined the older children in the obstacle courses. When the lottery chose her name, she got her first taste of the simulators. Without any guidance or prior training, she simulated engineering, navigating, flying, powering, and mechanizing. She naturally excelled in flying. Space Force fast tracked her into the advanced pilot program. She spent time when not flying, learning the other disciplines.*

*Kote had been in the pilot program for a few years when they met. The older girl did not force Vace to prove herself before they spoke. Kote and she became fast friends, despite the age difference. The girls were well matched in skill. Together, they rose through the ranks. Both Vace and Kote captained their own ships. Kote spent a three week mission in exo-orbit while Vace was chosen for a different assignment. Perhaps Kote wasn't as happy for her as she thought then. Not that it really mattered anyway. It all ended the day everything went wrong.*

Trying not to think about her dismissal, Vace sighs. "Think happy thoughts," she says to the empty cell. "I'm not dying in here."

"Not if I have anything to do with it," a voice says.

Lifting her head, she says, "Tallo?"

"At your service, Captain." Keys jingle. *Click.* The cell door slides open.

Hurrying off the cot, she spies Tallo with his long black hair artfully tied down his back. "How'd you know I was here?"

Tallo smiles. "It's my business to know." A tremor knocked them into a wall. "Your friend spoke with the Commander. He wasted no time. Evacuations are in order." They run through the corridors.

"Kote says there's a Razor in column two-four," Vace says.

"Uh-huh." He pressed her against the wall. Officers hurried past. "She also had you arrested. Cinq had a better idea."

"Cinq, too?"

He smiles before they race into another metal maze. "We swore we'd follow you into the beyond. A crew needs a captain and a ship. A captain needs a crew and a ship."

"I'm not a captain anymore," Vace mumbles. Lights flicker. They run with their bodies pressing along the wall while another tremor shakes the facility. Emerging in the hangar, Tallo keeps Vace close to the wall.

"She sees everything," he whispers. "In here." They enter a storage room.

"Under the tarp, Captain." A woman holds up a brown corner over a pallet full of crates.

Vace hastily ties her hair into a self holding bun. "Good to see you here, Dennia," she says before slipping under the brown tarp. Positioning herself between supply crates, she crouches.

"This is the last one," Dennia says.

"I'll make sure everyone is aboard," says Tallo.

"Hold on, Captain. We're moving," Dennia says in a low voice.

Vace jerks a little when the pallet begins to move. Activity flurries beyond the tarp. Dennia must be pushing her through the main hangar. Vace imagines every ship being called into service.

The pallet gains speed. Voices shout. She grasps the edges of the crates. The pallet stops. She holds her breath.

Lift gears grind. She rocks gently against the crates. Movement stops, then slow rolling.

Her dark cocoon is lifted. "Welcome to our new home," Dennia says. She helps Vace off the pallet.

Vace drinks in the metal cargo space of the ship. "Is this a Tantrum?"

"The only one," Dennia replies. She leads Vace through the ship. "When the other one crashed, they decommissioned the Tantrum series. This one has been grounded ever since. It's not being used for evacuations. We commandeered it."

Dennia opens a door. "Your quarters," she says.

Her eyes immediately find a uniform laying across the bed.

"Thought you may want to change."

Walking to the bed, Vace says, "This is an admiral's uniform."

"It's *your* admiral uniform," informs Dennia. "You were getting promoted that day." Turning, she continues, "I'll see you on the bridge."

Vace picks up the blue uniform. She sees her name in embroidery. Her fingers run over all her bars and admiral epithets. She smiles. Beside her bed rests her rucksack. Someone rescued it from Kote's office. She pulls her radio out of the rucksack, then places it on the bed.

After changing, she carries her radio like a talisman through the corridors. Ghosts of the sister ship claw at Vace, but her radio repels them. The hollow frantic screams almost seize her before reaching the door to the bridge.

The door opens, revealing a full crew. "Cap—Admiral on the bridge," someone announces. The crew stops to salute her.

She momentarily forgets to breathe. "As you were," Vace says.

"Admiral Vace," says Dennia, "the Tantrum is almost ready for launch. Cinq is in the bay."

"Let's finalize prep," Vace says. Both women leave the bridge.

Walking with Dennia, Vace's mind floats elsewhere. The alarms. The escape pods.

*A skeletal test crew accompanied her maiden test flight of the other Tantrum. They had just broken through Thelta's atmosphere when the first alarm sounded. The engineers aboard couldn't find the problem. Orbiting Thelta, then docking at Quint had to wait. She burned the thrusters to turn them around. The hull cracked. She barked orders. "Lock all doors. All personnel to escape pods." Cinq defied her commands.*

*"Get off the bridge, Cinq," Vace told her.*

*"I'm not leaving you, Captain. Something is not right," Cinq said.*

*"We're going to break apart upon re-entry," Vace yelled. "I will not have a death on my watch."*

*"What about you?"*

*"I can take care of me," Vace said. "Go!"*

*Cinq hesitated. "Captain, leave the ship," she advised.*

*"You know I can't do that."*

*"Your life is more important than protocol."*

*Vace stared at Cinq. "Go. That is my final order."*

*"Good luck, Captain." Cinq ran, leaving Vace alone.*

*Once the last pod escaped, Vace redirected life support and artificial gravity to the fire shields. She covered her nose and mouth with the auxiliary breather.*

*The Tantrum violently shuttered. More alarms rang as pieces of the ship separated from one another. Orange encapsulated her vision.*

Vace and Dennia slam to the floor. "Tremors," Vace mutters.

"They're getting worse. I hope Cinq is finished," Dennia says. The women pick themselves up after the shaking subsides.

After a few minutes, they walk into a secondary hold. "Admiral on deck," announces Dennia.

The crowd, both uniformed and plain clothed, salute Vace. Cinq stands in front of her. "Nice to see you again, Admiral Vace. We are filled to capacity with Space Force and civilians," she reports. "We are only waiting for Tallo."

Vace nods. "Thank you, Cinq." Cinq steps aside. Scanning the crowd, she does not spot Halkin. She hopes he evacuates in time.

"Welcome to Tantrum," she addresses the crowd. "This will be our new home for... well, until we find another. The tremors will continue to escalate and we will feel them until lift off. Time is not with us. Secure your belongings and strap yourselves in. Intercoms will be on throughout the ship. Everyone will be able to hear what I say from the bridge wherever you are. We will meet again soon. You are all dismissed."

The crowd disperses. "Admiral," says Cinq, "four other ships have agreed to follow your lead over Admiral Kote."

She stares at Cinq. "How did you manage this?"

"Lines were drawn when we discovered that Kote sabotaged your test flight," Cinq answers.

"She what? How is she an admiral?"

"Lack of sufficient evidence," Cinq replies. Her face scrunches in disgust.

"Tallo!" Dennia calls. Two men walk up the ramp into the ship.

"Done," says Tallo. "Kote is angry. The sooner we get airborne the better."

Vace looks at the man holding a rucksack behind Tallo. "Halkin," she greets.

"They shut down Sector three-three," Halkin says, "but it won't do us any good now. There's no more time. The people on the other side of the world have a better chance than we do."

"Close her up and make her hum," Vace commands. "Halkin, you're on the bridge for your expertise. Someone, get this man's belongings secure."

After a crewmember takes Halkin's rucksack, Dennia and Halkin follow Vace to the bridge. "What's our status?" Vace barks.

"Engines are firing," someone answers.

She sits in her commanding chair. "Get me online with the other ships in my fleet."

"Fleet captains ready."

"This is Tantrum," Vace says into the coms. "What are your statuses, Captains?"

"Warming engines," the four reply in succession.

"Exit hatches are open," Vace informs her captains. "Prepare for lift off. Watch for tremors. Evasive maneuvers if necessary."

"We're ready, Admiral," says Dennia.

Vace secures her radio to her control panel. She turns the dial to static. "This is Admiral Vace," she announces over the general coms with a wide smile, "Tantrum is taking off."

"You are not authorized for take-off, *Admiral*," answers Kote's voice.

"Not asking for authorization, Kote," Vace retorts. "Just extending a courtesy to the ships in the area."

Her hands rest on the controls. "Firing thrusters." The ship shakes with another tremor. They roll out of dock into the exit column. "Increasing speed for short ascent."

"But, Admiral, the column—"

"When the ground is moving, it doesn't matter how long the column is," Vace explains.

"This is Captain Farlon. Razor One, Fantam Squad is taking off," a voice announces over the coms.

"This is Captain Zine. Thorn, Fantam Squad taking off," another voice says.

"This is Captain Penka. Razor Two, Fantam Squad taking off."

"This is Captain Orlo. Seed, Fantam Squad taking off."

"Seeds have been grounded," Kote's frantic voice says. "I repeat, Seeds have been grounded."

"This is Lieutenant Commander Craileg," says a new voice over the general coms. "Seed Two, Fantam Squad taking off."

Smirking, Vace says, "Add Craileg to squad com. Gear is up."

"Craileg added."

The Tantrum floats through the launch column. "Cruising at hover speed," says Vace. "Increasing speed at regular rate for extraction."

"Fire in the column! Fire in the column!" Tallo alerts. "Twenty clicks behind us and catching."

Vace notices daylight ahead of them. "Pressing full speed," she says as calmly as possible. The static of her radio focuses her. "Daylight five clicks. Ready shades."

"Shades ready," someone answers.

"Fire ten clicks," Tallo reports.

"Light three clicks," Vace says.

"Fire five clicks."

"Light two clicks."

"Fire two clicks."

"Light one click."

"Fire one click," warns Tallow.

The ship passes the edges of the column. "Column clear," announces Vace. She steers the ship up sharply. Fire spits out of the column below them.

"The Woodlands are ablaze," Dennia says.

The ground vomits fire. Plumes of thick smoke billow. Vace says, "Fantam Squad, break atmosphere as quickly as possible."

Eruptions echo. Quiet sobbing fills a corner of the bridge. "Faster," Halkin urges.

Screens flash red. Alarms beep. "Thelta's blowing. Rocks fast approaching," alerts Cinq.

Vace spins the ship, dodging what she hopes is only rock or rubble. They duck around more rocketing debris. Something beside them explodes.

"Was that one of ours?" someone asks.

"No. Not our squad," replies another.

"They're all one of ours," Vace answers. She keeps her eyes on the smoke choked blue sky. "Come on," she breathes.

"Thelta's breaking up," Dennia says. Awe and sadness carry in her tone.

Vace wipes a budding tear from her eye. She weaves the ship around rubble, fireballs, and gushing smoke.

Clouds fade. Thelta gently curves against the black. Breaking through the soft glow, space envelops the ship. Quint blinks beyond them. The Anthro made five pointed star shaped space station watches the destruction about which it orbits.

"Fantam Squad," Vace commands, "keep flying. Do not slow down until well after Quint."

All five ships acknowledge.

The last of the ships break dock with Quint. Vace peeks through the ship's rear cameras. Black dots race to escape the orange inferno.

*Her sensors failed. They burned up upon re-entry. The shaking made her hand slip off the controls more than once. She held on. She had to keep the nose down or else she'd skip right off the exosphere and ricochet into space. Her head slammed into the seat multiple times. "Don't pass out," became her mantra. Sweat rolled down her skin.*

*The orange ended in white. The cloud cooled her.* "Space Force Command, come in," she said. "Captain Vace calling Space Force Command. Come in, Space Force Command."

*She heard nothing. No static. No breaking. Nothing. The coms were dead.*

*Crash landings happened in simulators. She had no idea where she was or how fast she was going. All she knew was that her instrument panel didn't work and getting caught in the clouds was disorienting at best. To make it home, she had to fly under the cloud level.*

"Quint is asking for pickups, Admiral," someone mentions.

"Has anyone answered their call?" Vace asks.

"Yes, several have set course for the space station."

"We will not dock at Quint, but prepare to pick up escape pods or stragglers," orders Vace.

A low rumble crescendos throughout the ship. "What is that?" Dennia asks.

"Thelta," Halkin answers. He does not turn his head to look.

Vace dares to look back. Molten yellow replaces her beautiful green planet. "Halkin," she barks, "why is Thelta yellow?"

"That's bad," he says. "Gases from within the planet are mixing with the atmosphere. Combustion levels should be starlike. And like stars, flares and eruptions and storms are possible."

"Tallo, can you make her go any faster?" Vace asks over the coms.

"I'll see what I can do," he answers.

Closing her eyes, Vace puts her faith in the metal shell to protect them.

*She flew out of the cloud only to find herself surrounded*

*within a city of clouds. She navigated around fluffy white spires, searching for an opening or at least a thinning in the layer. The badly damaged ship had to land soon.*

*After an hour of avoiding clouds, she plunged. The grayish white unsettled her. She hoped she held the nose at the same angle. Stories of pilots being turned upside down while flying through clouds gnawed at her. Believing she kept course, she also had to believe that her course would not end in her blowing up a mountain or slamming into the ground while shrouded in fog.*

*The cloud eventually retracted its grip on the spaceship. Green leafy treetops gently rolled out before her. Anthros lived, worked and played under those treetops. The branches that grew only at the tops of the trees interwove so thickly that she had no inkling of what lie beneath. And cutting even one branch was a punishable offense. Too much sunlight would penetrate the ground and the Anthros' delicate skin.*

*"This is Captain Vace with Space Force. Does anyone hear me?"*

*Nothing.*

*"Anyone? Please?" She changed frequencies. "Hello? Can anyone hear me?"*

*More beeping echoed through the bridge.*

*"If anyone can hear this, Tantrum is going down. I'm going to crash into the trees. I can't stop it. But, I will try to minimize impact damage. Captain Vace out."*

*Looking at the layer of green, she tried to gauge the best entry. A Tantrum was one of the larger ships in the Space Force fleet. The design allowed the ship to carry a crew into deep space for a long voyage. It was mainly for exploration and scant scientific research. The Tantrums were to precede the Seeds, which were being developed for extensive research and colonization. Vace was used to piloting Razors—smaller, agile ships capable of reaching other planets in their solar system for short journeys. She wondered if the Tantrum would have a similar maneuverability.*

*The damage to the rear and sides resisted the angle she tried to position the body of the ship. It was the only angle allowing minimal tree destruction. Breaking through the canopy would have to be as small as possible.*

*Green smacked the window. Wood cracked. She lowered the sunshade. The ship spun between the widely spaced trunks.*

*Grappling the controls, she attempted to steer the ship to a relative clearing. Everything beeped. The harness unlatched.*

*Seconds before impact, Vace let go of the controls. Her feet pushed against the panel. The chair unlocked. Spinning it around, she crouched in the seat. The back of the chair smashed into the control panel. Metal groaned.*

*She smelled a mixture of tar and rotten fish. And burnt fibers. She climbed out of the chair.*

*The window was in perfect condition. It had no weak point she could exploit. The door between the bridge and the rest of the ship buckled. It would not open. A floor panel had popped open during the crash. Prying it off, she dropped into engineer access. The dark, tight space has little walking room left. She crawled across an opened tool kit. She grabbed what she thought she could use.*

*Daylight peeked through the side of the ship. She slithered*

119

*toward it. With the screwdriver and hotgun, she worked it open enough for her to slide out.*

*Her bruised body fell to the damp ground. Roars and groans reached her ears. She raised her head. Many different colored flames caressed and pierced the hull. They reached for the trees.*

*Stumbling to her feet, she ran for help.*

"We now have fifty-two percent more speed," Tallo announces over the coms.

"Talk to the other squad lead engineers," Vace says. "See if they can gain more speed."

"Yes, Admiral."

"Increasing to new top speed," Vace says. She glances behind them. The yellow swallows some black dots.

"The fireball is growing," relays Dennia.

They push past Quint. "Staying course. Flying directly away from Thelta," she says to everyone and no one in particular. "We have cleared the outer moons' orbits."

"The moons are on the other side of the planet," says Halkin. "We should be at an okay distance."

"Heard, Halkin," Vace says. "Reducing thrusters twenty percent."

"The yellow is shrinking," says Dennia.

"It's burning out, or at least burning back," explains Halkin.

"Reducing speed an additional thirty percent," Vace informs. "Fantam Squad, report."

The five ships report an all clear.

"Fantam Squad, get in formation. Tantrum at point," Vace says. "Dennia, show us Thelta."

The fire engulfed rock that used to be their home burns on

every screen. Gasps, crying and non-repeatable choice words echo through the ship and over the coms. Other ships stop to watch the obliteration of Thelta from a safe distance.

Since eight years old, Vace always wanted to leave Thelta and explore worlds beyond. However, in all her dreams, coming home was never... not possible. Tearing her eyes away from the screen, she studies the others gawking at the destruction. She feels their sadness, their horror, their detachment. They are, after all, floating in space without an anchor. They have each other. They are not alone.

Staring out the window, the expansive darkness stares back at her. Insignificance overwhelms her. Static crackles on the radio. Smiling, she remembers finding that radio in a dejected corner of a forgotten storeroom a few weeks after she arrived at Space Force. It always brought her comfort when she felt like an insignificant cog in the machine. She heard that phrase on the radio, too.

"Admiral," says Dennia, "what do we do now?"

"Here is as good a place as any," the radio relays. Everyone on the bridge stares at Vace's old radio. Static returns.

The beyond calls.

"We have two Seeds in the squad," Vace says. "We link all six ships. Fantam Squad will become a community. This—these ships—is our home now. Someday, we may find a more permanent one. Tantrum will be the steering ship for the community, as we journey to parts unknown. We have witnessed the end of Thelta. But, it is not the end of Anthros. Our place in the universe will be found. Our story has just begun."

Vace answers the call.

# THE DEMON ON THE MOUNTAIN

## Larry Ivkovich

O n the second star-rise of her Death-Vigil, Maya encountered the Sky Demon. She thought perhaps the
Demon's image was a vision, brought about by her
illness, the heat of the Orange Barrens, and the fasting and sleep
deprivation she had undergone.

But, no, this was different somehow.

She knelt in a cleft between the Shoulders of Nortonon. The
rocky bluffs were sacred to the Qynda, and, hidden in its shad-
ows, Maya awaited the next stage of her people's life Journey.
Dressed in a long, white pilgrim's robe and ceremonial head-
wrap, she slowly forced herself out of her self-induced trance.
The trance helped to ease the pain of her affliction but she
wanted to be alert now. She wanted to see the Sky Demon fully
before she died.

Roosting cawthers had alerted her she was not alone. Bursting from the top of Nortonon's Peak, the birds' noisy flight broke through the fog in her shrouded mind. There, on the craggy mountaintop just above, glinting red in the light, she saw something move.

A figure. A man. But surely not a man.

He seemed oblivious to her presence, standing on the peak and gazing out over the Orange Barrens that served as home to her people. He looked young, certainly younger than Maya, with a Qynda-like face hidden by what seemed to be a beard and topped by long, braided black hair. The clothes he wore over his rugged frame were strange—short pants and ankle-high boots, a sleeveless shirt ripped and stained. Small pouches hung at his belt. He cradled some kind of long device in his arms. A weapon, perhaps?

As he turned to look over her hidden vantage point within the Shoulders, Maya trembled at the sight of something alien covering part of his dark face.

*A Sky Demon*, she thought, her old heart fluttering in her chest. *So, the ancient tales are true.*

She pulled herself painfully from her kneeling position on the prayer blanket, using the sides of the cleft as leverage. Once on her feet, she had to pause for breath. The familiar headiness of earth and vegetation filled her with their comforting scents but her vision swam as she closed her eyes and leaned against the rock. When she had recovered sufficiently, she looked back up to the peak but the figure was gone.

Her old eyes squinted in the light of the morning-star. The blue sky was cloudless this day, only cawthers and the rare asthawk traversing its azure breadth. She walked slowly around the cleft to the bluff's ridge, looking outward at the bordering ring of mountains that enclosed this end of the Barrens. Toward the east sprawled the Mouth of the God, the gorge's twisting, jagged depths opening like a raw cut in the earth. Opposite yawned the Grazing Hole, a gap in the mountains, which led to the sheltered scrublands beyond where the wild reina herds gathered. And there, located like the third point of what her old teachers had described as a "triangle," lay her home—the *communa* of the Qynda.

Carved into the dry foothills, the communa's ground dwellings and streets radiated outward from the central temple like a starburst. The tallest structure in the communa, the temple's peaked roofs and gables reached toward the sky. Six small domes, each painted a different color and representing the Stages of the Journey, nestled among the spires.

Houses and shops lined the symmetrically arranged streets and alleyways. The higher level of cliff dwellings, etched and sculpted out of the orange rock walls, loomed over the communa proper, their windows like watchful eyes. Tented stables were home to the desert reina, both precious beasts-of-burden and spiritual companions for the Qynda. Sand hens, the communa's main source of meat and eggs, scratched for food in specially-constructed pens.

Patches of green grass and rainbow-hued flowers contrasted with the orange rock that made up most of the village's construction. Within the circular wall that surrounded the village's lowest level, well-tended plots of root vegetables and grains and small but hardy fruit trees stood strong against the heat of the morning-star.

*I helped plant and cultivate those gardens,* Maya thought sadly. *My children and theirs will care for the next ones.*

A noise behind her... She turned and gasped, putting one fragile hand to her throat. Was she dreaming after all? The Sky Demon stood a short stone's toss away. Holding the long device pointed at the ground, the Demon's one visible eye roved over Maya's thin body. The other eye was hidden, covered by...

A mask. Now, this close, Maya could see that what she thought had been an alien thing was instead a mask covering the upper left half of the Demon's face. But it was like no mask she had ever seen. Metal with an eyepiece pulsing in blue light, it filled her with dread.

*Well,* she thought, collecting and holding onto the shreds of courage that threatened to scatter at any moment. *Nortonon knows I wanted to see him, didn't I?*

He approached her slowly, perhaps curious, but with a definite air of weary boredom uppermost in his manner. His skin was as brown as the earth itself, his body trim but dirty. And what Maya had taken to have been a beard was tattooing, a scarification of some kind drawn in intricate whorls and designs. He wore a bandage on one of his shoulders. It looked wet with blood.

He touched the mask with two fingers, inclined his head and then spoke. Maya's eyes widened in surprise. He spoke the language of the Qynda! Only then did she realize she was trembling. She held onto the Shoulder's stone tightly to keep herself from falling.

"Gentle Fem," the Demon said and then paused, head forward again, as if listening to some inner voice. "Aged Mun," he continued in her people's traditional greeting for one as advanced in years as she. "What in Vanera's name are you doing here?"

"I... I attend to my Death-Vigil," Maya answered, holding her head up. "You are the intruder in this place. What are *you* doing here?"

The Demon smiled.

When Maya discovered she had the wasting-sickness, she began to make plans for her passing through the Veil. The preparation for the final stage of her life's Journey required her to finish all earthly business, to see to the welfare of those she would leave behind, to give up all of her possessions and compose her entry into the Qynda's Book of the Veil—the communa's record of all who had passed through from this life to the next.

The Healing Wife could do no more for her. Maya was quite tired of drinking the pain-soothing mixture (its foul taste enough to make her even sicker!). The communa's Headman, Duranjaya, had released her of any debts or obligations she might owe to the Merchant Guild. The Priestesses of the temple had given her absolution and Nortonon's Rites of Clear Passing. Kaipo, her life-partner, was long dead. Her friends were few in these later days, she having lived well beyond most of them. Only Kasim shared her company. The frequent visits by the young basket-maker were the only bright spots for Maya anymore and soon, those too would end.

Her offspring, though, were another matter.

"Mun-Maya," her first-born, Aolani, said. "You have been honored. I don't mean to be cruel but you must realize that Kasim is not family."

*He has been more family to me than you ever were.* Maya sat in the Women's Tent, weaving the ceremonial head-wrap she would wear during her Death-Vigil. She wished Aolani would just go away. She had not been a particularly attentive daughter. Now, the only reason she was here was to make sure she was bequeathed some goods or property that would be handed down by her mun.

"Yes," Maya said softly, trying to hide the distaste in her heart. "Having the wasting-sickness is indeed an honor."

"An honor that only befalls a few of us, that only family can..."

Maya stood up too quickly, her anger barely controllable. She grasped one of the wooden pillars that supported the root-fiber roof, trying to hide the sudden dizziness that came over her. "Enough, daughter," she gasped. "Leave me now! I have no time for this. You will get what is coming to you, of that you need have no fear. But whether Kasim receives any of my possessions is my decision and none of your business! Now go!"

Aolani resembled her father, a reminder doubly painful to Maya. Thin and dark with long wavy hair, Aolani possessed, however, none of Kaipo's good nature and kind disposition. *She is too much like me,* Maya noted to herself with irony. *That is why we have never gotten along.*

Aolani pulled her cloak's hood over her head as she turned to go. "We will talk of this again, Mun-Maya," she said stiffly.

"You must see the reason for not giving our family's relics away to just anyone."

*Would that I could give you away*, Maya thought bitterly as she sat back down on the rock-hewn bench which encircled the fire pit. Incense burned slowly and sweetly in the flames of the women's sacred fire, illuminating the large interior of the tent with a shimmering, unearthly glow. The smoke drifted upward through the tent's roof aperture, the light of the even-star filtering through in fractured beams of muted radiance.

Maya closed her eyes against a sudden onslaught of pain. *An honor, yes, so they say*, she thought. *And yet, I have lived a long life, longer than most with this affliction. Most of those who get the wasting-sickness do so when they are much younger. Surely for them it is a curse!* Yet the sacrifices made to Nortonon in the form of the wasting-sickness' chosen ones kept the deity pleased. If Nortonon was happy, the deity shared good fortune with the communa.

So it had been throughout the Qynda's history in the world. Every generation, a few would get sick. The Healing Wives would tend them until determined it was indeed the wasting-sickness which had struck. Then ritual and duty would take over.

*I follow the same set pattern*, Maya thought again. *I've lived long and well. Why is it then that I am so bitter? So hollow inside?*

Maya's eyes fluttered open. She gasped, throwing her arms out to her sides. She lay on her prayer blanket, in the cooling shelter at the deep end of the Shoulders' cleft. What had happened?

Then she remembered the Sky Demon.

She sat up quickly, ignoring the sudden rush of dizziness that struck her. Struggling to her knees, she looked out of the cleft. A dark line of storm clouds simmered at the far horizon. Even at this distance, a flash of lighting caught her eye. *The rainy season approaches*, she thought absently. *But it's early this cycle as the priestesses foretold.*

At that moment, she saw the Demon.

He stood with Royan, her old and faithful reina, the loyal beast culled from the wild herd beyond the Grazing Hole when only a colt. Per custom, the Death-Vigilant would be accompanied by no one but her mount, allowing the reina to roam freely over the Shoulders' grass-covered bluffs until the moment of the vigilant's passing. By some instinctual urging, the mount would return to the communa at that moment, its appearance heralding the death of the individual so honored to be taken by Nortonon.

Maya hadn't seen Royan since she had loosed the reina upon arriving. But now, here he stood, only a few arm lengths away. Stranger still, the Demon held the animal's head in his hands and was... talking to him? *Royan does not fear him*, Maya thought in wonder. *What kind of demon inspires no fear?*

As if hearing her thoughts, the Demon turned his frightening gaze to her. "Ah, Aged Mun," he said in that strong, rich voice of his, a slight accent edging his words. "You've not left us yet, I see, though you slept for a long time." Indeed, Maya could see the morning-star had risen well past the nooning.

The Demon took something out of one of the packs on his

belt and held it out to Royan who instantly gobbled it up.

"What... what did you feed my mount?" Maya asked shakily. "Have you bespelled him? Will you sacrifice him to your dark gods?"

The Demon chuckled, pushing back his long hair away from his shoulders. "Bespelled? Sacrifice?" Another laugh. "I'd forgotten how primitive and superstitious some of you Outreach settlers are." He held something out in his hand, blue and box-shaped. "It's just a sweet-cube," he said, popping it into his own mouth. "All equines throughout history have relished them. I keep them for my own craving and it'll do your mount no harm, believe me. My people are descended from a horse culture so I know these animals well, if only through old history vids and data-crystals." He paused, looking up at the sky. "As far as serving dark gods, well, it may be true at that."

Maya realized her long white hair hung freely around her bony shoulders. She put her hands to her head, shooting a shocked look toward the Demon.

"You fainted," he said calmly. "The wrap was very tight, too tight. I took it off to give your scalp some breathing room. Plus I think seeing me probably gave you a little shock, eh?"

"That is against custom," she protested, trying to gather up her hair around her. "What will you do with me now that you have shorn me of my wrap and shamed me?"

The Demon held up one of his hands. "Nothing, old wom-an!" he said irritably. "Vanera curse these fragging primitive myths! I'll not interfere with your absurd Death-Vigil! You want to die here alone—have at it!"

With that he turned, gave Royan a final pat, and walked

away toward the banked escarpment that led to the peak. Royan nickered softly and ambled over to Maya, nuzzling her chest. Maya held onto the reina's strong neck as she watched the Sky Demon climb the peak. *A strange demon*, she thought, puzzled. *Not at all like the priestesses describe. What did he say—Out... Outreach settlers?*

Something happened to Maya then, something she hadn't felt in many a cycle. Curiosity overwhelmed her, curiosity and a burning desire to learn something new before she passed through the Veil. An opportunity had presented itself—a Sky Demon was here! She had talked to him; he had touched her! So little out-of-the-ordinary happened to the Qynda—theirs was a life of tending to their plantings and searching out water and other necessities and performing the necessary rituals and ablutions cycle after cycle. No other communas existed anymore that they knew of, though there were stories of such. Theirs was a gentle, patterned existence.

And dull and repetitive at times. Maya had never felt such excitement as she did now! Surely such a moment as this should be recorded and passed on. The Priestesses and even Nortonon himself would forgive her for such a lapse, surely. This was important. She would die at any rate—what difference when?

Leaning down to pick up her head-wrap, she began to shuffle to where her supplies and Royan's tack had been placed within the cleft. Death-Vigilants were permitted to bring a limited amount of food and drink with them. Maya hadn't touched hers yet, wanting to hurry her Journey's last stage, but she would now. She needed to be stronger for what she intended to do.

She sat down in the cooling shade of the cleft's hollow and opened her supply pack.

After she had eaten and drunk (and felt better) she discovered a corked skin of pain-soother in the bottom of her pack. *Kasim,* she smiled wryly. *This is his doing.* She took a deep breath. *Very well,* she thought. And then added as an afterthought, *Nortonon forgive me.*

She unstoppered the skin and, closing her eyes against the vile-tasting liquid, forced the draught down.

Only four star-risings earlier, Kasim had climbed the steps of the cliff dwellings, a strung-together sampling of baskets slung over one muscular shoulder. From her quarta window, Maya watched the craftsman approach, her position as one of the elders of the communa allowing her the privilege of living cliffside (though, at her age, the climbing of the stone steps inset into the cliff face was a dubious "privilege" at best).

*He has been like a son to me,* she thought, watching Kasim's dark, handsome form, clad only in short pants and sandals, his tied-back hair trailing down to his waist. *And I am grateful. But if I were younger...*

Kasim looked up toward her dwelling and waved, his smile almost as brilliant as the midday-star. Maya waved back, hoping he couldn't read her mind and that she would not be sick as she had been on Kasim's last visit. Then her roiling stomach had given up her morning meal, embarrassing her and making Kasim uncomfortable. She knew the basket-maker felt more sorry for *her* but she wanted to be at her best when he came calling.

She met him at the entrance to her quarta, bowing in traditional greeting to a visitor to her home. He returned the bow, removed his sandals and entered with his load of baskets.

"Blessings and joy to you, Fren-Maya," Kasim said cheerfully, though his dark, piercing eyes held a hint of sadness to belie his outward mood. "It has been three star-risings since last I saw you. I've been busy in my shop preparing for the Temple's Rain Festival. An early storm is foretold. How are you faring?"

"Better, I think," Maya lied, gesturing for him to have a seat. Maya's dwelling was simple—a circular living area carved out of the cliff face, replete with potted green plants grown by her own hand, two root-fiber chairs and a table arranged on a large torecat-skin rug with several reina-hide cushions lying about. Her walls were covered with chalk paintings Maya had done herself—depictions of the Qynda and, lately, the Six Stages of the Journey. "And blessings and joy to you as well, Fren-Kasim."

A small food storage and preparation room branched off to the rear of the main living space although most hot meals were done in the group cooking pits where everyone joined in with the preparing of the communa's foodstuffs. A rock-hewn stairway led to a small second level where Maya slept and maintained her personal shrine to Nortonon.

A rare, cool breeze blew in through the round windows. Maya had made sure to burn some incense in several locations throughout her quarta. Sometimes the stink of her sickness could be more than noticeable.

Kasim unstrung one of the baskets, holding it out to Maya. "For you, Aged Mun," he said, his dark-as-night face lighting up. "A gift from my heart, made by my hands."

Maya drew a quick breath of surprise. The basket was small but beautiful. Most craftsmen created their wares in a mostly utilitarian fashion—strong and useful. Kasim did the same but he was an artist first, fashioning his baskets to be pleasing to the eye. This one had asthawk feathers, shaped and formed to cover the basket's root-fiber shell, with colored gemstones inset along the rim. The handle was thin and gracefully curled.

"Kasim," Maya breathed as she took the basket and ran her hand over its silken surface. "You didn't have to do this. It is lovely." She looked at her young friend. "My thanks to you."

Kasim nodded, a glimmer of a smile on his lips. "I wanted you to have something special before you attend your Journey's final stage."

Maya started. "My final stage. How did you know? As yet, I've told no one except Aolani and the priestesses."

The craftsman shrugged. "I just knew. After my last visit, I sensed a finality in your manner, an embracing of your fate. Despite your sickness, you seemed at peace somehow. I've spent the last three star-risings working on this. I give it to you now to show how much you have meant to me."

"Oh, Kasim." Maya leaned forward and placed her hand over the craftsman's. "I was going to tell you, of course. I wanted to leave while I still have the strength and won't need to depend on anyone else. I don't want to be a burden. It's my time. I am being called to pass through the Veil."

"As we all will be called in time," Kasim said. "You are lucky to be so honored in your passing, having lived this long. I just... well, I'll miss you." The young artist's eyes filled with more of the sadness Maya had noticed moments before. "You more than anyone have been interested in my art and my skill with design," Kasim continued, a slight tremor to his voice. "You paid attention and asked questions when no one else cared for my aspiring to create more than just *useful* things. Because of that the Artisan Guild has finally accepted me into their ranks."

Tears came to Maya's eyes. Kasim had become an important part of her life, but she hadn't known that she had been fulfilling the same role for him. He certainly had his pick of eager women and chose readily. What did he need Maya for? He was just being kind to an old woman, surely, perhaps missing his own mother who had died so young. She squeezed his hand tightly and allowed him to take her into his arms in a gentle embrace.

"I'll miss you too," she whispered as she clung to him, feeling the youth and energy in his strong body. But Kasim was wrong—Maya wasn't at peace, she hadn't embraced her fate. She felt as if her time here, despite her age, was being cut short, that there was something more she had to do. Something important.

*But what?* she thought, her heart filled with sudden anguish. *Nortonon help me, I don't know what it is.*

Darkness had fallen and the even-star shone full and ripe over the encircling mountains when Maya found the Sky Demon. It was later than she thought. Had she slept so long again? She had to stop for a moment, leaning against an outcropping and breathing heavily. Despite the food, drink, and pain-soother she had consumed, the walk up the escarpment had taken its toll on her sickly body.

The Sky Demon sat on one of the rocks jutting from the bluffs on Nortonon's Peak affording a clear view of the Barrens, the Mouth of the God, and the Grazing Hole. Some type of artificial light illuminated him and his "campsite." He held a small square object in his hand while another strange device sat on the flat rock in front of him. Rectangular and about a forearm's length tall, the metallic tower supported a red crystalline orb, pulsing softly. For some reason, the idea of a "hearth" or "cooking pit" flashed through Maya's mind. A few arm lengths distance sat a stack of containers of some sort—boxy with strange flashing lights on their surfaces.

The Demon turned in her direction. The blue light covering his right eye blinked rapidly. For a moment, she shrank back at the sight. "Aged Mun," the Demon said, stepping off the rock and walking towards her. "Forgive my rudeness earlier. Vanera knows I'm not the most patient of men."

"What is that... that mask you wear?" Maya pointed a shaky finger at the Demon's face, putting as much force into her voice as she could. She had decided to take the offensive. Her time was short after all and she had nothing more to lose. She wanted to know what this demon was doing here! The Qynda might be in danger!

He smiled again. Maya realized that despite the mask and tattoos, the smile lit up his face handsomely. "This is a bio-implant," he said cryptically as he touched the mask. "It's equipped with translating software and helped me to stay in touch with my, uh, ex-partners as well as keep track of what the

137

Galactic Nexia is up to. Granted, it's an older model. The newer ones are much smaller and less cybernetic-looking but I like the style of the older one better. Makes me look, uh, somewhat fearsome." He paused for a moment, a far-away look in his one eye. "Plus it helps me to forget what I once was."

*Demon words.* "Yes. I see," Maya said, trying to bluff her way through the confusing litany. "What is it you do here then?"

The Demon folded his arms across his chest, cocked his head to one side and seemed to study Maya. "You have courage, old woman. I'll give you that. Most primitives would be scared witless in a situation like this. But enough about me. I have a few questions of my own."

"No! I demand to know..."

"Why are there no cats or dogs or even *reptans* here in your communa? It's true, isn't it?"

Maya blinked, taken aback by the question. "I... I do not understand your question," she said, puzzled. "What are you saying?"

"Domesticated animals, that is, besides your reina and sand hens. Pets. Your ancestors would have had some when they made planet-fall here or at least the genetic material and equipment to clone them."

Maya stared, wondering if she had already died and was hearing the voices of those who had gone beyond to the other side. Was she still lost in her trance? "Your words are meaningless to me," she said, her heart beating hard in her chest. "My, the Qynda's, ancestors were brought here by Nortonon, the great deity of all things, countless cycles ago to escape the Plague from their home world."

The Demon shook his head, his body, backlit by the unnatural light, seemed more shadow than man. "No," he said. "This is an Outreach settlement, one designated by the Galactic Nexia as tapped out resource-wise and unprofitable. It's supportive of nothing and off-limits because of some natural cataclysm or hazard. High surface radiation level, I wager, judging from the preliminary survey reports I've accessed. You and your people were brought here by the starliner *Andre Norton*, sponsored by the Kindred New World Corporation which was some kind of privately-funded settlement cadre."

*Kindred,* Maya thought, puzzled. *Qynda?*

The Demon looked intently at Maya. "Have you no written or oral history to be passed on or, at least, to help your people remember? I've researched this planet a little on my hand-held and through my implant network the last couple of hours."

"We have the old tales and the scrolls of the temple."

"Hmmm." The Demon looked thoughtful. "No doubt those have been corrupted through the centuries also. Here's what happened—the *Andre Norton* ran into trouble transporting its crew and passengers to their new homeworld and crash-landed here instead over six hundred years ago. There was some political blowup involving Kindred and by the time anyone found out about your ancestors and mounted a rescue, it was too late. The settlers had all been contaminated and this sector of the rim had been cordoned off because of a war going on at the time. After that, you were all just basically forgotten."

"No!" Maya felt dizzy but not from the wasting-sickness.

The words the Demon spoke unsettled her. "You lie!" she cried, anger bubbling to the surface. "You're trying to trick me, to curse me. You're a Sky Demon, an enemy of Nortonon! It is what the old tales and the priestesses tell us!"

She wobbled a little on her feet. Amazingly, the Demon came closer and steadied her. She felt a thrill at his touch, not one of fear but one associated with experiencing something completely beyond her ken. It was strangely exhilarating.

"Here," he said, quieter and oddly gentle in his manner. "Come sit down over here. I think we need to talk, eh?"

Maya allowed herself to be led to where the Demon had been sitting although the idea of experiencing such company as his was something she and her people had only experienced in nightmares. *What have I been chosen for?* she thought, partly in confusion and partly in wonder. *Surely this is not happening by chance?*

The unnatural light and the intricacy of the Demon's tattoos played tricks on her vision. He looked concerned, almost worried as he knelt in front of her. That could not be. Sky Demons didn't worry. They *caused* such emotion in others.

"How old are you?" he asked finally after looking at her for what seemed a long time.

"What does my age have to do with anything?" The defiance Maya felt only moments before was beginning to wane but she continued to resist. There was a puzzle here she needed to know the answer to.

"Just tell me. Something I discovered through the implant network."

*Implant network—a channel to his dark gods, this "Vanera" whose name he invokes.* "Sixty-two cycles. I've been blessed. Most of the Qynda don't live so long though not all get the wasting-sickness as I have."

The Demon sat back on his heels. He looked surprised, almost shocked as if he had been struck across the face. "That old," he repeated softly. "The solar year here is the same as Old Earth's and yet you've survived this long."

More strange words. Maya felt her anger returning. "Why do you do this? Why are you here?"

The Demon hung his head for a moment as if lost in thought. "I'm not a demon," he said, looking away. "I'm a man just like the ones in your communa."

"But you come from the Sky and speak our tongue!" Maya protested.

The Demon laughed, shaking his head. "That's my translator at work. You speak a devolved mish-mash of Galactic Basic—English from Old Earth. You're Earthan like me, although from the look of you, I'd say you were of pre-Contact Tahitian or maybe even ancient Hawaiian descent."

Maya stared, aghast. What was he saying?

"So not everyone here contracts the wasting-sickness?" the Demon asked, abruptly changing the subject.

"No... no," Maya muttered, looking away and then back again. "Only those, like myself, honored to be taken by Norto-non as sacrifice. It has always been so."

Another thoughtful look crossed the Demon's face for a moment as if he pondered mysterious celestial matters. And then, "I ran into some of my own trouble during my most recent smuggling run," he said. "Which gave me a reason to finally get out of this business. I thought this planet would be a good place to hide. You know out here on the galactic rim in a quarantined Outreach sector of space. So I landed my flitter, my sky craft, here."

A recent memory unfolded within Maya's mind. *Kasim said he saw a falling star two eves ago*, she thought, a sudden chill tickling her back. *Those celestial fires grace our skies so rarely. Could it have been the Sky Demon's... flitter?*

The Demon cast a sidelong glance at the bandage on his shoulder and then looked back at Maya, a strange, unreadable expression on his face. "And here I find you and your people while I'm waiting for my ex-business partners to give up searching and write me off so I can start over somewhere else." He shook his head. "Vanera works in mysterious ways, that's for sure."

"Please," Maya said, her anger giving way to confusion as she sensed her world was about to change. "I do not understand."

The Demon stood, turned and walked to where the stack of containers sat. He knelt and Maya could see him pressing the blinking lights on one of the boxy things with his finger in some sort of pattern. There was a hissing sound and the lid of the container opened slowly as if by magic. Mist curled from within as the Demon reached in and pulled something out—two thin round discs, soft-looking, and made of some unrecognizable silvery material.

He closed the box, pushed the lights again and came back to once again kneel in front of her. He peeled some transparent film from around one of the discs and then pressed the disc onto Maya's upper arm. The disc adhered as if covered in root paste.

Maya jerked in alarm as she felt a sudden warmth spread from her arm and start to work its way swiftly through her whole body. "What...?" She tried to rise but the Demon held her gently with both his hands.

"No need to worry, Aged Mun," he said. "Be still for a few heartbeats. These medicinal patches are what I've stolen from my ex-partners—combination pain neutralizer and cell rejuvenator. Bastards were hoarding them all for their own use."

Fear enveloped Maya. She struggled in the Demon's strong grasp. "What are you doing to me?" she cried. "Stop! Nortonon help me!"

Something was indeed happening to her, but something completely unexpected. The heat from the "patch" wasn't hurting her. In fact, it possessed a quality that she could only think of as... soothing.

Maya ceased her struggles. The pain in her body was receding. She felt stronger. Her stomach's constant upheaval had calmed. The Demon released his hold upon her as she looked at him in astonishment.

"It's not a cure," he said as if reading her thoughts. "But regular applications will keep the cancer at bay."

"Cancer?" Another demon word.

The Demon nodded, squatting back onto his heels. "That's what your wasting-sickness is called in my world."

Maya looked at the Demon as if with fresh eyes. "What... what are you?" she asked. She was feeling better by the moment.

The Demon sighed and looked away again as if afraid to meet her open stare. "I used to be a med-tech," he said. A slight smile curled his lips. "A 'medicine man', as my ancestors used to say, and I was pretty fragging good at it. But after yet another war, the Nexia regime changed and I refused to follow it, instead thinking smuggling would allow me to strike back." A hard look twisted his features.

Here in the even-star's light, the Demon's mask shone with reflected glimmerings. The blue light pulsed slowly as if in rhythm to the Demon's words. "The same old story. Like cancer—politics, racism and greed have never been completely eradicated in the known universe. The Galactic Nexia and its corrupt offshoot, the Rim World Conglomerate, have seen to that. People will never change."

Maya stood up carefully, feeling the strength in her legs. She stretched the kinks out of her age-worn body as if she had been asleep for a long time. She looked at her hands as if for the first time, felt her face and then directed her incredulous gaze at the Demon. For some reason she understood him now. His words made sense. Was the patch giving her knowledge as well as health? She found herself fascinated, wanting to hear more from this strange man even as she began to feel well for the first time in many a star-rising.

For he had told her the truth, she knew then. He *was* a man. But none like she had ever known.

"Then you fell from your Vanera's grace?" Maya asked.

Another sigh. "You could say that. It's a long story," he said, a note of sadness in his voice. "Aren't they all? I got into smuggling after I'd bugged out of the Nexia Medical Corps." He laughed, a short, barking sound. "It became just all about the money and surviving at any cost." He stopped, spearing her with a desperate look. "To my shame, I realize I'd become just like the Galactic Nexia. Even by stealing the medicinals, all I've thought of since is how much profit I can make."

"Can you help *us* then?" she asked, realizing this was what she was here for—to speak for her people. "Can you help the Qynda? If what you say is true, we will benefit. *We* need these... medicinals! Can you not give some to the communa as you have done to me? To stave off the wasting-sickness?"

"You don't understand," the Demon said, moving close to Maya, his face only a hair's length away. She smelled his sweat, his stale breath. "If my ex-partners find out where I am, they won't go easy on me. They'll hunt me across the galactic rim if necessary. And if the Nexia agents track me here, if they find out I've messed with a local planet's culture in any way, despite its Outreach status, then I'll really be in deep crap! I'll be fragged from both ends! I need to find buyers who have real finances, real money, who can make this worthwhile for me, to allow me to really disappear for good."

"So you are indeed only concerned with profit, nothing more. You are afraid to do otherwise." Maya found herself becoming agitated again at the Demon's words. His revelation of his true cowardly nature rubbed her raw. "A demon who fears. You would let your gods so ruthlessly control you?"

A harsh laugh. "I said you wouldn't understand. How could you? You know nothing about me except what your 'old tales' tell you and those aren't even true! And look at you—devolved, primitive."

Maya bristled. "I know what fear is and what it does to people!" she exclaimed. "And to think I feared *you*!"

Maya backed up, startled. Not at her bold and presumptuous

outburst but at something she glimpsed over the Demon's shoulder, out in the Orange Barrens. She ran to the edge of the bluff, looking towards the distant Grazing Hole where now, above it, dark storm clouds had gathered. The light from the even-star illuminated something coming through the gap in the mountains.

Maya looked hard. Her aged sight could suddenly pick out distant details like a young girl. A herd of wild reina, stampeded in fright, their eyes wide, their leg muscles pumping furiously. And on their backs...

"Parket's Glimmering," she breathed. "I've heard it spoken of but never thought I would see it." Thin ribbons of flashing light curled and arced from the backs of the reina like wriggling rock serpents, giving them the appearance of living fire.

The Demon stood beside her. She heard him grunt in surprise. "Some kind of ball lightning or static electricity," he said. "I've heard of this too. It's a variation of what the ancient Earthans called St. Elmo's Fire. The atmospheric conditions have to be just right."

A sharp tingling danced over her, the short white hairs on her arms rising. She looked to the west beyond the cliff dwellings where more storm clouds had appeared. In the even-star's light, they roiled and churned, approaching swiftly from where she had observed them earlier. Much too swiftly. "The herd runs in panic because of the Glimmering," she said, turning to face the Demon. "And they're headed for the Mouth of the God. If they aren't turned they'll fall to their death!"

The Demon looked at her, his one eyebrow raised in question. "The reina are our brothers and sisters!" she cried. "Our spiritual companions and lifeblood."

"Because they survived like you and flourished," the Demon finished with a nod. "The cats and dogs and other animals didn't make it but the reina and the hens did, just like some of the indigenous flora and fauna have adapted. The torecats and cawthers, for example. You and they survived whatever contaminant pollutes this world. Hey!"

On an impulse, she grabbed the second patch from the Demon's hand and started running back down the escarpment. Maya had no more time for talk. She must act!

"Old woman!"

Maya turned and looked back at the Demon. "What's your name?" he asked. She told him. "I want to help, Maya," he said in a suddenly small voice. "But I... I..." He stood, as if he wanted to say something more, but then just looked away.

*He can be of no help,* Maya thought sadly as she turned from him and continued running. She knew the Demon, revealed now as weak and indecisive, possessed no special powers after all. He was only a man with his own troubles, trapped by his own failings who cared for nothing except what he could gain for himself.

She found Royan nervously mincing and eager to run. *He senses the herd's plight,* Maya thought. *And feels the oncoming storm.* He trotted to her and she mounted him without blanket or bridle. There was no time. Wrapping her arms around his neck and gripping his sides tightly with her legs, she cried, "Go, Royan! Fly, my brother!"

Royan took his head and paced down the winding back path of the Shoulders of Nortonon that led to the Barrens. Maya hung on tightly, feeling Royan's powerful muscles moving beneath her. The reina darted down the pathway swiftly but carefully. With Maya's guidance, her mount maneuvered around rocks and fallen tree limbs, clinging to the mountain's side to avoid the open edge that dropped down to the rocky surface below.

The thickness in the air was more noticeable now as the storm got closer. The crackling sensation felt earlier was more pronounced as both Maya's hair and Royan's mane began to twist and undulate with the beginnings of the Glimmering. Maya's skin crawled with a strange prickling. An aura of wispy fire surrounded her and Royan's every movement.

They reached the bottom of the peak, the Orange Barrens spread out starkly before them. Maya looked toward her home. Her fellow Qynda were awake; light-orbs and torches lit up the communa. Those she knew—Adrian, Kylie, Fortuna, Kasim, Duranjaya the Headman, and others—would be readying their own reinas to pursue the herd.

She looked back at the stampeding beasts. *They are too far away,* she thought. *They'll never get to the herd in time. We're the closer. It's up to us.* "Go, Royan!" she cried in her mount's ear. "Run!"

The reina sped up, his old muscles somehow reaching back and finding the power of his youth. Maya had run Royan many times, but never like this. It was as if the reina knew there was danger, that his fellow creatures needed help. He raced toward the front of the herd, Maya whispering directions and encouragement and holding on for her life.

But Royan was galloping crosswise against the wind now as a gale heralding the oncoming storm kicked up. Maya struggled to hold her mount on course. The aging reina surged forward, his neck outstretched, his mane flying, his legs pounding the earth.

They neared the herd and... there! The lead stallion, an imposing young male, black as night, led his charges on a panic-stricken course straight for the Mouth of the God. To Maya's right, the Mouth gaped like a giant maw in the even-star's light, ready to swallow the herd in one gulp.

She dug her knees into Royan's flanks, urging him on. Royan cut in front of the herd and charged the stallion, pulling up alongside him through clouds of dust and dirt. Wide-eyed with fear, the stallion turned his head toward Royan, bared his teeth and screamed a warning.

Royan backed off, momentarily intimidated. This close, the Glimmering was even more frightening, tangles of whipping fire leaping and dancing off of the reinas' backs. Sudden small sparks appeared in Royan's mane.

Maya coaxed him on again, knowing her mount couldn't keep this pace for much longer. If the Glimmering formed around him, he would lose all courage as his wild fellows had.

But the stallion would not relinquish his misguided control. He lashed out, his teeth snapping at Royan's face. Royan's head reared back as he neighed shrilly. Again he slowed, not able or willing to challenge the younger stallion. *He is tiring,* Maya thought in alarm. *Nortonon help... No! Not Nortonon!*

Maya risked a look back upwards toward the deity's mountain. "Demon!" she cried into the wind. "Help us!"

As if in response to her plea, a thin, straight beam of blue light miraculously speared outward from the top of the peak. Maya followed its path as it shot past her and struck the lead stallion. The stallion cried out and stumbled! He began to slow, falling back into the body of the herd. But he recovered and began to regain his ground. Again, a second beam flashed out and hit him in the neck.

Shaking his head, the stallion faded back into the herd, visibly weakened but not sorely so.

"Go! Now, my brother!" But Maya's mount struggled, his old body failing at the end. Some of the herd were overtaking him. *No!* she thought. *Not now!* Her right hand inched upward to her face—within her clenched fist she still clutched the Demon's second patch. Royan didn't have the wasting-sickness, she knew. But perhaps this alien thing could give him the extra strength he needed, as it had done to her.

She worked the covering film off the patch with her teeth and slapped the device against Royan's shoulder.

A moment passed, a heartbeat.

Suddenly, Royan neighed and jumped forward, almost spilling Maya to the ground. Like a young colt, her mount sped to the front of the herd, turned his head and cried out over his back to his fellow reinas.

Maya gripped tighter, praying she could hold on. Her own aged body was starting to weaken as well. She hadn't ridden this hard in so long. She looked to the gorge ahead of them. The Mouth of the God was right there, just ahead.

Maya dug her knee into Royan's right side and pulled on his mane on the opposite, directing him to the left. The left! Royan began to move in that direction. The herd swerved with him, obeying their new lead stallion. Slowly, slowly... The gorge was to Maya's right side now. She looked back. The entire herd followed, away from the Mouth and back towards the Grazing Hole! Through the clouds of dust, Maya could see torches approaching. Her friends and neighbors from the communa were near.

*We have done it!* she exulted. And then, she remembered the long device, the weapon, the Demon possessed, the beam of light striking the stallion. *The Demon helped us. He helped us!* She squeezed Royan harder, tears spilling from her eyes. She looked up then as a sudden darkness fell—the storm clouds had passed in front of the even-star.

Thunder boomed and the skies opened up.

Kasim had to pry Maya's hands from Royan's neck and her knees from his sides. She gripped her mount so hard she thought she would crush him. But once she was on the ground, barely standing on shaky legs, Royan nuzzled her once, turned and bolted for the herd, now back in the scrublands on the other side of the Grazing Hole.

"Maya, you did it!" Kasim put his arm around Maya's shoulders. "Praise Nortonon. You saved the herd!"

It still rained, but gently now, the worst of the storm having quickly spent itself. Maya stood leaning against Kasim, drenched, her white hair a tangled wet mess hanging limply about her shoulders. Tired and weak, she felt rejuvenated nonetheless, a feeling of health and power coursing through her. Absently, she touched the patch on her arm.

"That thing…?" Kasim began, his handsome brow furrowed in thought.

"It is a wonder," Maya said, grasping his arm. "The Qynda must know of this!"

"Yes. But there is something you have to see."

Maya frowned. "What is it, Kasim? What's the matter?"

In response, Kasim took Maya's hand and led her away from the Grazing Hole entrance toward the opposite end of the scrublands. As they walked, other members of the communa rode amongst the herd, seeing to its welfare, making sure none of the wild reina were hurt or still fearful. The Parket's Glimmering had gone, washed away by the storm but the herd was docile, almost welcoming the Qynda's presence. She saw Royan trotting with the black stallion, both reinas tossing their heads and nipping at each other playfully as if old herd-mates.

Around a rocky outcropping, several hands taller than both Maya and Kasim and pointing its sharp angles toward the sky, Kasim stopped. "Look," he said.

Maya gasped. One of the cloth-covered containers in which the Demon stored his medicinal patches floated in front of them, hovering two or three hands above the ground like a flitter-bug. It hummed softly with some internal workings as the lights on its front panel pulsed and sparkled.

"I found it here as I was looking for you and Royan." Kasim's voice was steady but Maya sensed a nervousness behind his words.

"You didn't tell Duranjaya?" she asked, looking intently at her friend.

"I… I was going to but…," Kasim shrugged. "I don't know

why but I did not. You and Royan appearing out of nowhere to save the wild ones and then this thing appearing? I suspect there is a connection. I thought you should see this first."

Maya nodded, understanding but not revealing anything yet. She bent down cautiously, noticing another object clinging to the side of the container—another box-shaped device, small but possessing the ever-present glowing lights. She moved in for a closer look.

"No! Maya!" Kasim grasped her to pull her back but Maya resisted.

"This is not a bad thing, Kasim," she said gently. "It is a gift from Nortonon." She turned and knelt, peering closely at the small device.

A sudden light flashed from the device, bathing Maya in its blue radiance. "Voice ID confirmed," a spirit voice said from nowhere. Maya stared, spellbound, as she heard Kasim gasp behind her. And then, another voice sounded from the air, a voice she knew.

"Maya. This is Samson Nakai." A pause. "The Sky Demon."

Kasim drew in a sharp breath. Maya sat back on her heels, her hands clenched at her breasts.

The voice of the Demon Nakai continued. "During all the confusion, after you rode that herd like some ancient Wild West vid hero, I had a fragging epiphany."

*Epiphany. Still he speaks in Demon words,* Maya thought. *Yet I think I know what this one means.*

"As you can see, I've left a storage case," the Demon continued. "There are enough patches for you and whoever needs them among your people for about two or three months. Moons, that is. Apply them once every seven star-risings. There should be enough to last until I get back with help. And, Vanera willing or not, I *will* be back!"

Maya leaned forward. "Can you hear me, then?" she asked. "You will truly return?"

The Demon Nakai's voice went on. "I'm going to muddy my trail here a little so the Rim World Conglomerate and my ex-partners will bypass this planet in their search for me; so the Qynda will be safe. It's not just helping you and your people—it's the fact so many of you have survived the cancer all these centuries. You said not everyone contracts it. If the cancer-fighting agent can be isolated in those that have survived or resisted the disease like you, well, we could finally have a cure after all this time, at least for your particular type of sickness." A laugh. "I may be all wrong on that point, but I promise you I *will* return. Just talk to the cold-storage safe. Yes, you heard me. It's powered by a small, voice-activated AI and will follow your commands. I changed the combination to open at your request also."

Maya gawked at Kasim in astonishment. Her young friend knelt beside her, a stunned look on his handsome face.

"I told you—you have courage, old woman," the Demon Nakai said. "You proved to me that it's about time I got mine back."

Silence. The voice ceased.

"Maya?"

Maya turned to her friend, her heart beating hard in her chest. "We must tell Duranjaya and call a Council," she said.

"We must convince them, all of the Qynda, of the importance of what lies inside this container."

Kasim wet his lips. "But what *is* the importance of it? What does all this mean? How do you know a... a Sky Demon?"

Maya rose to her feet unaided. "I will tell you, Fren-Kasim," she said, holding out her hand to him. "I will tell everyone that the next stage of my Journey must wait a little longer."

Maya and Kasim jerked their gazes skyward—a fiery orb, a flitter, flashed across the sky in streamers of light. *Farewell, Demon Nakai,* Maya thought.

Four and a half moons later, in the waning star-risings of the vernal season, the Sky Demon returned. Two of his flitters descended through the clouds and landed gently at the outskirts of the communa. Maya was there to meet the Demon along with Kasim, Duranjaya and a few others chosen to represent the Qynda.

It was early, the Orange Barrens glowing softly in the light of the morning-star, a rare breeze whispering coolly over the groups' cloaked bodies, the sky full of clouds. Patches of wild flowers, dormant during the long dry season, sprouted and bloomed. *I will write about this in my entry in the Book of the Veil,* Maya thought proudly. *It is a day for all Qynda.*

She sat in a litter constructed by the men of her communa, wrapped in reina hide blankets. The Demon Nakai's patches had helped several of her people but though they had strengthened Maya and kept her living for far longer than she had a right to, her wasting-sickness was too advanced and was finally breaking her body down. No longer able to walk and barely able to talk, Maya still insisted on being here this star-rising despite the ravages of her illness. She had to see the Demon one more time.

Aolani stood at her mun's side, not for any love or emotional attachment, Maya knew. But Maya's once-again failing health had forced her into accepting her first-born's help. Now that Maya had been considered an aide to Nortonon, now that she had befriended a Sky Demon who was about to bring a great Change to their people, Aolani had latched onto Maya for the importance such a position entailed.

*So be it*, Maya thought. *What do I care now? Kasim will still get most of my property and possessions. There is nothing she can do about that.*

The flitters had dropped through the clouds like dragons from the old tales. Small and streamlined, the strange craft looked like solid, black teardrops lying on their sides.

An audible gasp sounded from the group as an opening appeared on one of the craft. Maya squinted to see... there! The Demon Nakai emerged with two others—a man and woman like him but different still. One was of the Demon's race with brown skin, high cheekbones—proud and fearless-looking. The woman's skin, like Kasim's, was the color of the darkest night.

From the second craft, two more figures emerged. One resembled some of the Qynda with fair skin and dark hair. His companion was as alien as anything described in the old tales, possessing green, scaled flesh and golden serpent eyes.

Maya felt a ripple of fear shoot through the congregation at the sight of such a creature but the group held its ground. It was too late to change their minds, to turn back, now. Pride for her people surged within Maya.

The four secondary demons stood behind at the front of their respective flitters while the Demon Nakai approached. He nodded to Duranjaya the Headman, Kasim and the others, but smiled broadly when he saw Maya.

"Old woman," he said. "Maya. It's good to see you again, gentle fem." He looked different, wearing a white, close-fitting uniform, headscarf and gloves like his four comrades. But his face...

Maya managed a thin smile. "You have your newer... implant, I see," she whispered in a soft, hoarse voice, appraising the small rectangle of light that glimmered on the Demon's temple. "Now I can fully appreciate the entirety of your handsome face."

The Demon Nakai chuckled, knelt in front of her and took her hand. Despite his laughter, sorrow glinted in his eyes. "I'm sorry. It took longer than I thought it would to get back here. And we're only here unofficially."

Maya held her head up. "I never doubted. I knew you would return."

The Demon nodded, smiling. "It looks like you were successful in convincing your people to accept that wild story about me. A Sky Demon indeed!"

Maya nodded, a sudden lump in her throat. It *had* been difficult. She and Kasim had talked themselves into exhaustion but finally, with reservations, most of the Qynda had decided to be a part of this great Changing. It had helped Maya's cause when several small, insect-like craft called "drones" began arriving at the communa with messages from the Demon Sakai. Still, some of her people had left, fleeing further into the Barrens, afraid and unsure. In the end, Nortonon would see to all their needs, no matter what.

Although, she knew, she wouldn't be here to experience most of what would follow this day. The next stage of her life's Journey had been delayed but not halted. She squeezed the Demon's hand.

"You're the reason for all of this, Fren-Maya," the Demon Nakai said. "You're the most courageous person I've ever known. I'll miss you when the time comes."

"And I you, Fren-Samson," Maya replied, her already-weakened voice quivering with emotion. "But I am not done yet!"

"Then let's get started!" the Demon Nakai cried, flashing Maya a brilliant smile. He stood up, hands on his hips and surveyed the congregation. Duranjaya and Kasim had brought gifts for the Demon but stood there now like all the others, transfixed and waiting.

"People of the Qynda," the Demon said. "I am Brother Samson Nakai of the newly incorporated Unified Brotherhood of Interstellar Hospices of New Earth." He smiled. "Unofficial, as yet, but we plan on changing that status soon enough."

He paused, studying the now rapt, attentive faces looking at him. "There's an old Earthan expression, a little melodramatic but appropriate, I think—'Today is the first day of the rest of your life.' With what we can accomplish here, we can not only help your people but the whole of the Galactic Nexia. What do you say we begin our research, eh? We have a lot of work to do."

Maya smiled and closed her eyes. She felt Aolani's hand on one shoulder and Kasim's on the other. Instinctively she grasped both.

The next stage of the Qynda's Journey had begun.

# ABOUT THE AUTHORS

## Fred Adams, Jr.

### ASTROTRASH

Fred Adams, Jr. is a western Pennsylvania native who has enjoyed a lifelong love affair with horror, fantasy, and science fiction literature and films. He holds a Ph.D. in American Literature from Duquesne University and recently retired from teaching writing and literature in the English Department of Penn State University.

He has published over 50 short stories in amateur and professional magazines and anthologies, including the story "Masks" in LHP's *Moonshadows*. He has also published hundreds of news features as a staff writer and sportswriter for the now *Pittsburgh Tribune-Review*. In the 1970s, Fred published the fanzine *Spoor* and its companion *The Spoor Antholoy*. His novels, *Hitwolf* and *Six Gun Terrors* were published in 2014 and his novels *Dead Man's Melody* and *Mobsters and Monsters: the Adventures of C. O. Jones* will be published in 2015.

# Timothy Bateson

## EVALINE TRANSCENDENT

Timothy Bateson is a displaced Englishman currently living in Alaska. His interests include falconry, history, role-playing and music. Since moving to Alaska in 2005, he has been honing his writing skills with short stories and outlines for his werewolf novel. Having been raised in London, and now living in America with his wife, Sandi, a fellow creative soul, he is familiar with living in two different worlds, helping him sympathize with his shapeshifters.

Working in retail helped him promote and sell out at his first book signing event. Timothy was one of the authors who organized, and participated in the 2015 Author Cyber Convention on Goodreads. His website has more information about upcoming events, his characters, his stories, and links to his blog and book reviews. TimothyBatesonAuthor.weebly.com Contact Timothy at timothy.bateson.author@gmail.com.

# Joseph Castellano

## ROAM

Joseph Castellano has a passion for formulating new ideas and concepts. He brings that creativity and energetic demeanor to his day to day. As a business owner, he strives for the pursuit of perfection. Joseph pursues perfection in the cockpit as well, being an active pilot. His aeronautical adventures afford him the opportunity to belong to multiple flying associations. On any given day, Joseph can be found at the dog park with his dog, Odinn, attempting to catch frisbees whizzing by his head.

Contact Joseph at Contact.JosephCastellano@gmail.com.

# IE Castellano

## SECTOR THREE-THREE

IE Castellano is an American author and poet living in the Eastern United States. After earning a Bachelor of Arts in Liberal Studies, she ventured into the world of penning fiction. She loves history (especially ancient), mythology, archeology, and anthropology. Anything IE reads, sees, or does could wind up in one of her books in some manner. With her propensity to ask, what if, she writes speculative fiction—authoring the space opera, *Where Pirates Go to Die*, the dystopian sci-fi novel, *Tricentennial*, and the contemporary epic fantasy series, *The World In-between*.

For news and a current list of her writings, visit her blog: IECastellano.blogspot.com. Contact IE at IECastellano@zoho.com.

# Larry Ivkovich

## THE DEMON ON THE MOUNTAIN

Larry Ivkovich is a former IT professional (with a Bachelor's Degree in Fine Art) who has been writing genre fiction for over thirty years.

His short work has been published in various online and print publications. He has been a finalist in the L. Ron Hubbard's Writers of the Future contest and was the 2010 recipient of the CZP/Rannu Fund award for fiction.

Larry's published novels include the urban fantasy *The Sixth Precept* from IFWG Publishing and fantasy adventure *Blood of the Daxas*, published by Assent Publishing. Self-published novellas are *Reunion at Olan* and *The Final Lesson*.

Larry is a member of the Pittsburgh Worldrights and WorD, two local writing and critique groups, as well as the statewide group Pennwriters. He lives in Coraopolis, PA with his wife, Martha, and two cats, Trixie and Milo.

inkfish1.wix.com/LarryIvkovichAuthor
LarryIvkovichAuthor.wordpress.com

www.ingramcontent.com/pod-product-compliance
Lightning Source LLC
Chambersburg PA
CBHW021015180626
46814CB00003B/1294